JAMES PATTERSON
BOOKSHOTS

Dear Reader,

You're about to experience a revolution in reading—BookShots.

BookShots are a whole new kind of book—100 percent story-driven, no fluff, always under $5.

I've written or co-written nearly all the BookShots and they're among my best novels of any length.

At 150 pages or fewer, BookShots can be read in a night, on a commute, even on your cell phone during breaks at work.

I hope you enjoy *French Twist*.

All my best,

James Patterson

P.S.

For special offers and the full list of BookShot titles, please go to

BookShots.com

BOOK**SHOTS**

FRENCH TWIST

A DETECTIVE LUC MONCRIEF MYSTERY

JAMES PATTERSON
WITH RICHARD DiLALLO

BOOKSHOTS

Little, Brown and Company

New York Boston London

BookShots / Little, Brown and Company
Hachette Book Group
1290 Avenue of the Americas, New York, NY 10104
bookshots.com

First Edition: February 2017

BookShots is an imprint of Little, Brown and Company, a division of Hachette Book Group, Inc. The Little, Brown name and logo are trademarks of Hachette Book Group, Inc. The BookShots name and logo are trademarks of JBP Business, LLC.

The publisher is not responsible for websites (or their content) that are not owned by the publisher.

The Hachette Speakers Bureau provides a wide range of authors for speaking events. To find out more, go to hachettespeakersbureau.com or call (866) 376-6591.

ISBN 978-0-316-46971-5
LCCN 2016957112

10 9 8 7 6 5 4 3 2

LSC-C

Printed in the United States of America

FRENCH TWIST

CHAPTER 1

"I HAVE ABSOLUTELY NO appetite! Absolutely none! So don't waste your money, Moncrief!"

This is Katherine Burke speaking. K. Burke is my NYPD detective partner and she is furious with me. This is not an unusual state of affairs between us.

"We're supposed to be on the job, and instead we're sitting in this ridiculously fancy restaurant having a thousand-dollar lunch," she says.

"But you have never tasted anything so magnificent as the oyster and pearls appetizer served here at Per Se," I say.

I raise a small spoonful of the appetizer and move it toward her.

"White sturgeon caviar, icy just-shucked oysters, a dollop of sweet tapioca and…"

"Get that food away from me," she says. "I am way too angry to eat."

"But I am not," I say, and I pop the spoonful into my mouth and put an exaggerated expression of ecstasy on my face.

Don't get the wrong impression. K. Burke and I are great friends *and* a great detective team. Our methods, however, are very different. Burke is a tough native New Yorker. She plays by the book—strict procedure, always sticking to the rules. I, on the other hand, believe in going with my instinct—feelings, intuition. By the way, I am a native Frenchman, Luc Moncrief.

These different approaches lead to occasional disagreements. They also enable solutions to very tough cases.

I eat my appetizer in absolute silence. Then I say, "If you're not going to eat yours..."

She pulls the plate back toward herself and takes a bite. If a woman is able to chew angrily, then K. Burke chews angrily. In a few seconds, however, her mood transforms into peacefulness.

"This time you are pushing things too far. It's almost three o'clock. We should not be sitting here still having lunch."

"K. Burke, please, if you will. Our assignment is completed. And I must remind you that it was an assignment that amounted to absolutely nothing. A complete waste of time. In any event, we did what we were told to do. Now we should enjoy ourselves."

I signal the waiter to pour us each some more Bâtard-Montrachet.

I am, by the way, telling K. Burke the absolute truth about the assignment. And she knows it. Here is how it all went down...

Per the instructions of our boss, Nick Elliott, we arrived at Pier 94 on 54th Street and the Hudson River at 5 a.m. Let me repeat the time. Five a.m.! When I was a young man in Paris, 5 a.m. was when the evening ended.

In any event, Inspector Elliott said that he had unimpeachable, impeccable, irreproachable information that the stolen parts of rare 1950s-era American automobiles—Nash Ramblers, Packards,

Studebakers—were being shipped to collectors worldwide, ingeniously smuggled into supply boxes for cruise ships at the 54th Street shipping pier.

We arrived (at 5 a.m.!) with detectives from Arts and Antiquities, four officers from the New York Motor Vehicles Bureau, and three NYPD officers with .38 Special handguns.

Beginning at 6 a.m. the officers, using crowbars and electric chainsaws, began uncrating large wooden boxes that were about to be loaded on board. Or, as K. Burke informed me, "laded on board." Apparently her second cousin was a longshoreman. K. Burke is full of revelations.

To no one's complete surprise, the crates marked "Steinway & Sons" contained pianos. The crates marked "Seagram's" contained whiskey. The crates marked "Frozen Ostrich Meat" contained…you guessed it.

By eleven o'clock we had uncovered properly tax-receipted crates of video games, mattresses, antacids, bolts of silk, *but* no automotive parts.

At noon I texted Nick Elliott and told him that we discovered nothing.

He texted back an infuriating, Are you sure?

I refused to answer the insulting question. So Detective Burke texted back, Yes, Moncrief is sure.

While Burke was texting Elliott, I was texting Per Se, making a lunch reservation. And that is where we now sit.

"You always make me sound like a hard-ass workaholic, Moncrief," Burke says.

"Hard-ass?" I say. "I think not. A little difficult. A little stubborn. But not a hard-ass. You are a woman, and because you are a woman…"

"Don't you dare say anything vulgar or sexist, Moncrief. I swear I'll report you to NYPD Internal Affairs."

"But I never say anything vulgar or sexist," I say.

Burke squints for a moment, puts down her salad fork, then says, "You know something? Come to think of it, you never do. I apologize."

"*Ce n'est rien.* It's nothing."

Burke lets a small smile sneak on to her face. We're aligned again. And that's truly important. Her friendship means the world to me. I've had a very bad year, to say the least. My beloved girlfriend, Dalia, died, and I was left with an impossibly broken heart. Shortly after Dalia's death my *not* very beloved father died. This left me with an obscenely large inheritance, but a great sum of money did nothing to repair my heart. Only my friend and partner K. Burke kept me sane through all of it.

Two waiters now swoop in and lift our empty appetizer plates from the table. Almost immediately two different waiters swoop in with our main course of butter-poached sable with a mission fig jam. The sable is accompanied by toasted hazelnuts and…

K. Burke's cell phone rings.

"I asked you to turn off that foolish machine," I say.

"Yes, you did, and I told you that I would not."

She looks at her phone. Then she looks at me.

"We are wanted at 754 Fifth Avenue," she says.

"Bergdorf Goodman, the store for rich women," I say.

"You got it."

"Well, we cannot leave before we are served our main course."

"Yes, we can. There's a dead woman in a dressing room at Bergdorf Goodman. Inspector Elliott will meet us there in fifteen minutes."

I toss my napkin onto the table.

"I know we cannot decline the job, K. Burke. But I am disappointed," I say.

She stands at her chair and speaks.

"Why not ask the waiter for *le petit sac pour emporter les restes*?"

"This is a French expression that *you* know and that I do not," I say.

She smiles broadly.

"Translation: a doggy bag."

CHAPTER 2

THE VERY EFFICIENT K. Burke calls for a squad car as I sign my Per Se house account receipt. The police car speeds us along Central Park South. In five minutes we are at Bergdorf Goodman.

We exit the squad car, and we both immediately realize that something very weird is going on. Burke and I are *not* greeted with the usual crime scene madness. There's *nothing* to indicate that a homicide has occurred inside this famous store. *No* flashing lights, *no* zigzag of yellow DO NOT CROSS POLICE LINE tape, *no* police officers holding back a curious crowd.

"What the hell is going on here?" Burke asks. "It looks so… so…not like a crime scene."

For a second I think we may have the wrong location. As if she could read my mind, Burke says, "I know this is the right place. But…let's go in and see."

Inside, the same thing. A busy day for the wealthy. Everything is calm and beautiful. Elegant women and an occasional man examine five-thousand-dollar handbags, perfumes in crystal bottles, costume jewelry as expensive as the real thing.

Our boss, Nick Elliott, is waiting right inside the entrance for us.

Elliott looks serious and concerned. His greeting is typical: "You two are finally here." Then he gets right to the point.

"Before I take you upstairs I've got to tell you something. This scene plays out like a typical natural death. A twenty-five-year-old woman, name of Tessa Fulbright, suddenly drops dead in a dressing room. Maybe a heart attack or a drug OD or a brain aneurysm. But it's not. It's a shitload bigger than that."

Elliott says that he'll give us the most important details upstairs in a few minutes.

"They gave me details in the car on the way over, but nobody thought to mention what floor it's on. Lemme check," Elliott says. He begins to punch into his cell phone. Before he gets the correct floor number, I speak.

"It's the sixth floor," I say.

Almost in perfect unison Elliott and Burke say, "How'd you know that?"

"Floor six has the youthful designer clothing."

They know what I am not going to say: I am remembering the days before Dalia died.

Two minutes later, with a store detective and a floor manager accompanying us, Burke, Elliott, and I are standing in a very large, very lovely dressing room. It is furnished with two armchairs and a small sofa, both of them upholstered in pale purple, the signature color of the store.

One other thing: there is a stunning, beautiful, red-haired young woman lying on the floor. She is wearing a Chloé summer gown with the price tag still attached.

Burke and I kneel and examine the body closely. Other than the dead woman's beauty, there is nothing unusual about her.

"I assume you noticed the tattoo behind the right ear," says Burke.

"The tiny star? We got it," says Elliott. Then he looks down at the deceased, shakes his head, and speaks to the small police staff around him.

"You can take Ms. Fulbright downtown. Don't dare release the body. She belongs to us until I say so."

The medical examiner nods. Then Elliott looks at me and Burke.

"Here's the deal," he says. "In the last two weeks there have been two other deaths *exactly like this one*. The first one was in Saks Fifth Avenue, ten blocks away."

Elliott explains that a twenty-three-year-old woman, Mara Monahan, died suddenly—literally dropped dead—while she was paying for shoes. Elliott and his teenage daughter were having lunch around the corner at Burger Heaven when the call came in. So after lunch, when Elliott's daughter took off, he went over to Saks to take a quick look-see.

"So this Mara Monahan turns out to be the wife of Clifton Monahan, the congressman from the Upper East Side. Maybe you've seen her picture online or something. This Mara Monahan is a beautiful, I mean *beautiful*, blonde."

"I heard about this," K. Burke says. "The *Post* and *Daily News* were having a field day with their covers. She was beautiful."

I interject. "I was at her table at the gala dinner for the Holy Apostles Soup Kitchen. She was a knockout."

"Could we refocus on the *pertinent parts* of the case, gentlemen?" Burke says.

"Anyway. I figure I'd better make nice to her husband, the congressman. I'll be under a crushing amount of pressure and scrutiny to close this case. So I go see him. He's broken up. Really broken up, I mean. Two days later there's a funeral. I go. Lots of big-shots. Cuomo's there, Cardinal Dolan does the service. Over and out. Sad stuff."

But there's one more chapter in Nick Elliott's story. He tells us that the following Monday, almost a week after the Monahan woman dies, a few days before today's date, a second-string Broadway actress dropped dead in one of the only restaurants in New York as expensive as Per Se. It's called Eleven Madison Park, and yes, the woman was young and beautiful and…

"Brunette this time," I say.

"No," Elliott says. "This one is blond, also."

One quick glance at Burke, and I can tell that she's pleased that my hunch was wrong.

Elliott explains that this woman is the understudy to the female lead in the latest Broadway smash hit. But, perhaps as a measure in case her acting career doesn't work out, the woman, Jenna Lee Austin, recently married a multimillionaire hedge funder. Elliott also points out that the medical examiner's reports in both deaths show no sign of trauma, *no* injuries, or, almost as important, no sign of any foreign substance in the victims' systems, nothing that could indicate a cause of death. And looking at victim number three here, she seems like she's going to match the pattern.

So, NYPD has three young, beautiful, rich women, all of them apparently dead from natural causes, all of them dead in the middle of an ordinary day in three of the fanciest places in Manhattan.

"What do you need us to do?" K. Burke asks.

"Frankly, everything. Hit the computers. Pull all the info on all the women, their husbands, their friends. The first one seemed like a tragedy, the second more suspicious, and now with three—there's obviously some sort of connection. And we don't have one goddamn idea what it is. So I want you two to take over from Banks and Lin, who are working the first two. See them and get caught up."

I nod. Burke gives her typically enthusiastic, "Got it, sir."

Elliott says, "I'll see you at the precinct tomorrow."

"A small problem, Inspector," I say. Then Burke jumps in.

"We have one of our rare long weekends. But we can cancel all that and come in to work."

I interrupt her quickly, almost rudely.

"No, we cannot," I say. "Detective Burke seems to have forgotten. We *do* have some plans for the weekend."

K. Burke looks slightly startled, but she is smart enough to know that she'd better trust me on this one.

"Okay," Elliott says. "Bang the hell out of the computers tonight. See what you can find. By Sunday you'll have the ME's report. I'll assume you two will be in on Sunday?"

"But of course," I say.

He nods to the store detective. They both begin to walk toward the elevator. Then Elliott stops for just a moment. His face has the barest trace of a smile. Then he speaks, "Have a good time." God only knows what he is assuming about Burke and me.

Nick Elliott makes his way through the sea of Carolina Herrera dresses and Stella McCartney jackets. Katherine Burke looks at me. Her eyes narrow slightly.

"Okay, Moncrief. What the hell is going on?"

"What's going on is this: I shall pick you up at your apartment tomorrow morning at 6. And please, K. Burke, be sure to bring some nice clothes. Yes, this case looks very interesting. But, my friend, so is this little trip that I've planned."

CHAPTER 3

VERY LITTLE TRAFFIC IN Manhattan. Very little traffic on the Hutchinson River Parkway. Very little traffic on Purchase Street. Everything is going our way. So, in thirty-five minutes K. Burke and I are walking through the Westchester County Airport in White Plains, New York.

Burke is, after all, a detective, accustomed to ridiculously early hours. So she is wide-awake and bright-eyed, and also a trifle confused. We walk through a small gate marked PRIVATE AIRCRAFT. I am about to show my driver's license to the security guard as ID, but the young man waves his hand casually and says, "No need, Mr. Moncrief. Welcome aboard."

Five minutes later we are in the sky.

"First question," she says. "What's with this fancy jet? Don't tell me you rented a private plane."

"No. I did not rent it," I say. "I bought it. It is called a Gulfstream G650, and it contains enough fuel to fly for about seven thousand miles. That's my complete knowledge of the vehicle."

She shakes her head slowly and says, "They should give one of these planes to every NYPD detective. It would make days off so much more fun."

Then she says, "Question number two. Tell me where we're going, Moncrief, or I'm walking off this plane."

"No need to prepare your parachute, K. Burke. We are going to a city named Louisville, in the state of Kentucky."

As I say the word "Kentucky," the attractive young woman who greeted us as we boarded crouches beside us, rests her hand on mine, and asks if we would like some champagne or coffee. (I hear K. Burke mutter, "Oh, brother.") Both Burke and I decline the offer of champagne and settle for a perfectly pulled cappuccino. As if the coffee was a magical elixir that filled her with special knowledge, K. Burke suddenly shouts.

"The Derby!" she says loudly. "Tomorrow is the Kentucky Derby!"

"Congratulations. You are a detective *parfaite,*" I say.

"Since when did you become a horse-racing fan? And please don't tell me you bought a horse and managed to get him into the Kentucky Derby."

"No, although I did think about it. But the dearest friends of my late parents have a horse running tomorrow at Churchill Downs. They have been racing horses ever since I can remember. Madame and Monsieur Savatier, Marguerite and Nicolas. The name of their extraordinary horse is *Garçon,* although his full name is *Vilain Garçon,* which means 'naughty boy.'"

"So, they named the horse after you," she laughs.

"An easy joke, K. Burke. Too easy."

"Irresistible," she says.

"In any event, the Savatiers have been in Louisville for two months while Garçon was training. For Nicolas and Marguerite the Kentucky Derby has been their dream. They have rented a house, and we will be staying with them. They will meet us when we land."

Burke and I each have another cappuccino, and less than an hour later we arrive at Louisville International Airport.

We exit the plane. At the bottom of the steps waits an elegant old woman wearing an elegant gray suit and a large white hat. Next to her stands an equally elegant-looking man of a similar age. He, too, wears a suit of gray. He also wears an old-fashioned straw boater. They both carry gold-handled canes.

"*Bienvenue, Luc. Bonjour, mon ami bien-aimé.*" Welcome, my beloved friend.

We embrace.

"*Madame et Monsieur Savatier,* I wish to present my best friend, Mademoiselle Katherine Burke," I say. "Miss Burke, Marguerite and Nicolas Savatier."

The three of them exchange gentle handshakes. K. Burke says that she has heard wonderful things about them as well as "your great horse, Vilain Garçon."

"*Merci,*" says Madame Savatier. "And I must say this. Since Luc just called you *his* best friend, that makes you also *our* best friend."

Monsieur Savatier speaks. I immediately recall what a stern and funny old Frenchman he can be.

"Please, everyone," he says. "This is all very touching. But we must hurry. In less than a half hour they will be having the final workout of the horses. And no friendship is worth being late for that."

CHAPTER 4

THE FIRST SATURDAY IN May. That's the date of the Kentucky Derby. May promises sunny weather. But today, May does not make good on that promise. The sky is overcast. The temperatures are in the mid-forties. The only sunshine is the excitement in the noisy, boozy, very colorful crowd. Katherine Burke, the Savatiers, and I are standing outside the super-elite Infield Club. This is where the horse owners and their friends gather. Here most women are dressed as if they are attending a British royal wedding: huge floral print dresses, most of them in bright primary colors; necklaces and brooches and earrings with sparkling diamonds, emeralds, and rubies. The women's hats are each a crazy story unto themselves—huge affairs that must be pinned and clipped to remain afloat, in colors that perfectly match or clash with the colors of their dresses.

The men are in morning suits or are dressed in classic-cut blazers—each a different rainbow color. Bright club ties, striped ties, bowties. The whole area has the feeling of happy anxiety and big money. And of course no one is without a smartphone, constantly raised to capture the moment. This has to be the most thoroughly photographed Kentucky Derby in history.

I give K. Burke two hundred dollars.

"Bet one hundred on Garçon for me, one hundred on Garçon for yourself," I tell her.

"I'm not going to take your money," she says.

"But this time you must. To watch the race with a bet riding on it makes it a million times more exciting. But I must prepare you for the worst."

She looks surprised.

"Garçon has little chance of winning. The oddsmakers have his chances at forty to one."

"I don't care," she says, in the true spirit of the Derby. "He's our horse." And she is off to the betting window. She's become a real racing fan.

K. Burke clutches our tickets tightly. She is dressed more casually than most of the women in the infield, but she looks enchanting. Marguerite Savatier has given Burke a piece of Garçon's silks—a red, white, and yellow swatch of cloth. Burke has tied it around her waist as a belt. She looks terrific in a simple white billowing cotton dress. And if anyone present thinks Burke is out of her social element, all they need do is glance at the huge emerald necklace, the gift that I gave her this past Christmas in Paris.

Then it is time for the race.

Grooms snap lead shanks onto their horses and escort them out of their stalls. Then comes the traditional parade. The horses are conducted past the clubhouse turn, then under the twin spires of Churchill Downs. Finally, the horses are brought into the paddock to be saddled.

Nicolas and Marguerite Savatier speak to Garçon's jockey and trainers. They save their most important words for…who else? Garçon. Both Savatiers stroke the horse's nose. Marguerite touches his cheek. Then they move away.

Now comes the moment that most people, myself among them, find the most touching. It begins with a simple, sad piece of music. A college band begins playing a very old Stephen Foster song. Everyone at the Derby sings along, right down to the heartbreaking final verse:

Weep no more my lady.
Oh! Weep no more today.
We will sing one song
For my old Kentucky home.
For the old Kentucky home, far away.

And the race begins.

For me there is no sporting event that does not excite me when I am watching in person. Boxing. Basketball. Tennis. Hockey. But nothing compares to horse-racing. And nothing in horse-racing compares to the Kentucky Derby.

It is even more incredible to be watching the race with owners of one of the racehorses. It is almost as exciting watching K. Burke transform from a no-nonsense NYPD detective into a crazed racing fan. She clenches her fingers into fists. She screams the word "Garçon" over and over, literally without stopping for breath.

And the race itself?

If I could have "fixed" the race, I am ashamed to say, I would have taken all of my father's inheritance and done so. Nothing would please me more than to see my elderly frail friends, Marguerite and Nicolas, break down in tears as Vilain Garçon crossed first at the finish line. Nothing would please me more than to see my best friend in her white cotton dress jump for joy, her emerald necklace flapping up and down. Yes, it would have been worth my fortune to see that happen.

As it turns out, I did not have to spend a penny.

The voice on the loudspeaker, above the cheering, came out shouting, with a perfect Southern accent, "And the winner, by half a length, is VILL-EN GAR-ÇON!"

CHAPTER 5

THE BEST THING ABOUT being the governor of Kentucky must be hosting the Winner's Party for the Kentucky Derby.

We watch the giant wreath of roses being placed upon Garçon. Then we head to the Kentucky Derby Museum for the Winner's Party. K. Burke and I are sort of maid of honor and best man at a royal wedding. We get to enter with the bride and groom, Marguerite and Nicolas. Shouts. Cheers. Music.

"I bet that most of the people here think that we're the son and daughter of the Savatiers," K. Burke says.

"Or the son and daughter-*in-law*," I say. Burke acts as if she did not hear what I just said.

Armand Joscoe, the tough little French jockey who is hugely responsible for Garçon's victory, is carried around the room on a chair, like a bride at a Jewish wedding.

"He's adorable," says K. Burke.

"When I was a lad everyone called him *Petit Nez*, Little Nose. He has been with the Savatiers forever. This win is a wonderful day for him."

"No more *Petit Nez* for him," says Burke. I now look at the commotion around the Savatiers.

The charming old couple is, as always, composed and courteous as they field the questions from society magazines, racing magazines, newspaper and TV reporters from all over the world, and gossip blogs. Marguerite's gentle voice is barely audible among the thousands of clicks from the cameras and cell phones. It is their show. Burke and I stand many feet away from the stars.

"Have you tasted the mint julep?" I ask K. Burke.

"I'm an Irish girl. I prefer my whiskey straight up," she says. "I just don't understand the combination of mint and bourbon."

As if on cue a waiter passes by with a tray of chilled mint juleps. I take two from the waiter and hand one to K. Burke.

"As a good guest and adventurer you must try the local drink," I say.

Reluctantly she says, "Okay." We both hold our drinks in the air.

"To Garçon and his owners," I say.

"To you, Moncrief, with a big thank you for this trip," Burke says.

"My pleasure, partner," I say. We clink. We sip. She speaks.

"Hmmm. I think I may have been wrong about bourbon and mint leaves. I could easily get used to this concoction," she says.

I frown and say, "Not me. A white Bordeaux will always be my drink."

"Over there," Burke says, pointing to a nearby waiter with a tray of good-looking hors d'oeuvres. Then she adds, "What do you think those things are?"

"Hush puppies with country ham," I say.

"I didn't know you were such an expert on Kentucky food," Burke says. "You're just full of surprises, Moncrief."

We are poised to grab a few bites from the hors d'oeuvres tray when the orchestra suddenly lets go with a musical fanfare. A commotion seems to be taking place in the area where the Savatiers are being interviewed and photographed. Always on the job, Burke shoots me a look and heads toward our friends.

As we push our way through the crowd, a spotlight hits the older couple. A gigantic arrangement of red roses is being carried in. It's even larger than the garland of roses that was draped on Garçon. The floral arrangement is so large that it takes four men to carry it. They place it in front of the Savatiers. Marguerite and Nicolas's heads disappear behind the huge red rose arrangement.

One of the unidentified four men holds a mic. It clicks on with a screeching noise.

"Five hundred American Beauty roses for one wonderful French woman," he says. His accent is tough, New York–ish.

Both Savatiers seem confused. The two Derby officials with the Savatiers also seem confused. The four men walk away quickly.

"Was that some official part of the winner's ceremony?" Burke asks.

I shrug my shoulders. "So much of what you Americans do is a little bit crazy. Let's go find the waiter with the hors d'oeuvres."

In the next hour Burke and I set some kind of record for "Most Hors d'Oeuvres and Canapés Consumed at Churchill Downs." We set a similar record for "Most Mint Juleps Consumed at Churchill Downs."

We are drunk enough to have trouble forming words when we kiss the Savatiers farewell. Our thanks are heartfelt and garbled. Fortunately, the Savatiers' chauffeur drives us to the airport. Moments later we are aloft. On our way back to New York. On our way back to the murders of the three beautiful young women.

I try to do some mental theorizing about the case. But I am tired, and my brain is muddled, and K. Burke's head is resting on my shoulder.

CHAPTER 6

KATHERINE MARY BURKE UNLOCKS the three dead bolts that will allow her to enter her apartment. After the door is finally opened, she surveys the one-room apartment on East 90th Street where she has lived for the past five years.

All those keys and locks to keep this little place safe. Is this cramped little studio even worth protecting? she thinks. The dark-green sofa, dotted with stains. It's the sofa that her cousin Maddy was going to throw out. The two needlepoint pillows that a friend made. The first one says, THERE'S NO PLACE LIKE HOME. The second one says, YOU CALL THIS PLACE HOME?

When she first rented the apartment it seemed spacious and bright. That was before she set up the fake-pine IKEA coffee table with the wobbly fourth leg. That's before she made the decision to keep the Murphy bed permanently opened and unmade. That's before the club chair from the Salvation Army became the *de facto* storage unit for her pile of shirts, jeans, slacks, and tights, plus an occasional shoe, boot, or sneaker.

Yet Burke came to love the place. It was simple. It was sweet. Most of all, it was hers. Okay, her best friend Moncrief may live in a loft big enough to host a basketball game, but life has a way of evening out sorrow and joy. She would never trade her simple life for Luc's wealthy world, a world scarred by death and tragedy. Sometimes she wonders how he gets through the day without crying.

And what the hell, right now Burke is feeling rich, too. The $4,000 she won on Garçon is the biggest single amount she has had since…since…well, since ever. She could pay her Time Warner Cable bill, she could buy a really cool first communion gift for her niece Emma Rose, she could bank some of it so that when Christmas came she could buy Moncrief something a bit fancier than a fake Cross pen and pencil set (which he did, however, keep on his desk and actually use).

Burke drops her luggage on the floor. Then she plugs in her laptop and her smartphone for recharging.

She unpins her hair and removes her bright silk belt. The juleps are catching up with her.

One last look at her e-mail. It has been a few hours since she checked it. There might be important info on the three murder cases that she and Moncrief are jumping on top of tomorrow.

Nothing urgent. Some new files about the victims' cell phones, no important DNA material from any of the crime scenes, a few useless pieces from the gossip sites TMZ and Dlisted about the alleged affair between Tessa Fulbright's husband and a twenty-year-old Yankees farm-team player. Hmm. He's in the closet? Interesting but probably irrelevant.

Finally, there is an e-mail from Mike Delaney. Mike is part-owner and weekend bartender at a place called, what else? Delaney's. Mike isn't the sharpest guy Burke has ever met, but…Mike is sort of like her apartment. Mike is simple. He's sweet. And she knows she could have him for the asking.

She falls backward on the bed. Her head hurts. Her feet hurt. But she is full of happy memories of the Derby, the roses, the party, the juleps…and a friend like Moncrief.

Friend. The word "friend" seems to stick uneasily in her mind. What do you call a male friend who's rich and handsome and funny, and when you accidentally-on-purpose fall asleep on his shoulder you feel warm and comfortable?

"I guess you just call it…a Moncrief," she thinks.

Then she falls asleep.

CHAPTER 7

"ALL RIGHT, I HAVE it entirely figured out," I say as K. Burke, wearing "I've-got-a-hangover" sunglasses, walks into the precinct.

"Can it wait five minutes until I put a little coffee in my engine?"

"K. Burke, it is ten o'clock Sunday morning. We agreed to meet at 9 a.m.? I assume you were not at church," I say.

"Moncrief, already you're making me crazy, so I'm going to give you my mother's two favorite words of warning," Burke says. "Two simple words."

"Please, nothing obscene," I say.

"Obscene? My mother? No way. Here are the two words." Then she shouts: *"Don't start!"*

I am stunned for a moment, but just for a moment.

"But why would I not *start?*" I ask. Then I launch into my analysis.

"There was no cause of death determined in the postmortem on the first two victims, but you have no doubt read the autopsy report from the medical examiner concerning Ms. Tessa Fulbright, the dead woman in Bergdorf?"

"No, I have not, but I'm sure you'll tell me what I need to know," says Burke.

"With pleasure. As we noted, there was no physical abuse, no bruising, no fractures. Beyond that there were no unusual substances in her blood…"

"Unusual? You mean like poison?" Burke says.

"Correct. Unless, like me, you consider a small amount of instant oatmeal and trace amounts of pomegranate juice to be poison."

"That's it?" Burke asks. I can tell by the wrinkled forehead and the speed with which she gulps her coffee that she's listening hard.

"Yes, that's it for the examination, but that's not the end of the information I have found. I called Tessa Fulbright's pharmacy this morning and received some interesting information."

"How'd you know what drugstore to call? From her husband?"

"No. But I figured it out easily. We knew she bought her wardrobe at Bergdorf's. So I correctly assumed that she bought her medicines at C.O. Bigelow, the most glamorous pharmacy in Manhattan. Tessa Fulbright did not seem like the kind of woman who would wait on line at Duane Reade."

"So what did you find out?"

"Not much. Not really much at all. She was due for a refill on Nembutal, which as you know is…"

It's K. Burke's turn to show off a bit.

"It's a pretty popular antidepressant, a pentobarbital pill-pop. You'd have to swallow an awful lot to kill yourself. Marilyn Monroe left town on it. Anyway, if it wasn't showing up in Fulbright's autopsy, I'd rule it out."

"*Moi aussi.* Me too, but, I am sad to report that the only other thing the postmortem examination showed in her blood was a high amount of sugar and a certain amount of a medication named…"

Here I pause and refer to my iPad for the name. "Dulcolax. It is a stool softener."

"I know what Dulcolax is," she says.

"Ah, so the hardened stool is a problem that you suffer from, K. Burke?"

"I'm not going to say it again, Moncrief. *Don't start!*"

CHAPTER 8

I AM, OF COURSE, laughing at my little joke. And I believe that she, too, is suppressing a smile.

"Okay," I say, almost ready to rub my hands together with enthusiasm, "Now for the big insight. Turn on your computer. I have something more to show you. Something important."

Burke quickly boots up the desktop and enters a code. She turns away from the beeping computer sounds as if they are making her head hurt.

"Okay, the computer's ready. I'm ready. What's up?" she says.

"Here's what's up!" I say, and in my enthusiasm begin very quickly calling up some pages on the screen.

"Alors," I shout. "Look at this."

She studies the screen for a few moments and then eyes me suspiciously.

"It's photographs of the three dead women," Burke says. She gives a short shrug. "So what? We have photos of…lemme see if I remember right…this is the redhead from Bergdorf, Tessa Fulbright. This one is the blonde who died in the restaurant. The 21 Club."

I interrupt. "No, *not* 21 Club, *but* there is a number in the restaurant name—Eleven Madison Park."

"Her name is Jenna Lee Austin. She's the actress. The understudy. Married to the hedge funder."

"*C'est magnifique.* Now. The final *Jeopardy!* answer is…?"

Katherine Burke does not hesitate. She taps the screen photo of the third victim.

"Mara Monahan. Shoe department, Saks Fifth Avenue."

"You go home with a million dollars!" I yell.

"Great," she says. "I'll just add it to the four thousand bucks from yesterday."

"And now I will show you something else," I say.

I quickly tap a few keys on Burke's computer. "See?"

Under the photo of each dead woman appears a photo of a different man. Beneath Tessa's photo is a strapping young blond lifeguard type. Under Mara's is one of those nerdy-handsome guys, the black eyeglass frames, the slightly startled smile. Under Jenna's photo is the "older gentleman," who looks amazingly like the former French Minister of Agriculture (but is not).

"Who are these guys? Their husbands?" K. Burke asks.

"A good guess," I say. *"Mais non."*

"Do I get a second chance?" she asks.

And then she knows.

"They're the boyfriends, aren't they?"

"Precisely," I say.

"How'd you figure it out, Moncrief? Instinct?"

"No, no, K. Burke. Not at all."

"Then how'd you find them?"

"On Facebook, of course."

CHAPTER 9

WHEN KATHERINE BURKE AND I go to work we really go to work.

On the sixth floor of Saks Fifth Avenue, where a simple pair of Louboutin heels can cost more than the monthly rent on a Sutton Place one-bedroom, we ignore the exquisite merchandise (and I ignore the smooth, sexy curves of the customers' legs).

"If you could just take us through the movements that Mrs. Monahan made as you remember them," Burke says to Cory Lawrence, the department manager. Young Cory looks as if he'd be right at home on a prep school tennis team or a Southampton polo club.

"Well, as I understand it from the store representative helping her…"

Burke interrupts, "That store representative is the same thing as a *salesman?*"

"That's right," Cory Lawrence says. He is not unpleasant, but his voice does have a touch of *you're obviously unfamiliar with the ways of fancy stores.*

"Okay, if you could walk us through it," I say.

Cory Lawrence speaks softly. He says that he would like to do this as quietly and unobtrusively as possible, so as not to annoy the "clients." "Clients" is apparently the new word for "customers."

"Okay, Mrs. Monahan tried on some shoes, made her choices, and then she slipped back into her Tory Burch sandals. I escorted her to the sales counter. Because she's a frequent, valued customer she has access to our exclusive app, available only to customers who spend a hundred thousand a year with us, where she can just pay with a tap of her phone. And that was it."

"Did she say anything? Did you have any sense that she wasn't feeling well?" Burke asks.

"No, not at all. She said something when the phones tapped, like 'Oh, this is like a little kiss.' Then I noticed that she stopped smiling. I was about to ask whether she wanted the shoes sent to her home, and...*bam*...she just sort of collapsed to the ground."

"What did you do then?" Burke asks.

"What did I do? I thought she had fainted. I touched her face gently. Her eyes were adrift. And then a young man—in a black Ferragamo suit, I couldn't help but notice—rushed over and began calling her name. Then there was store security, and we called 911. But then the EMT said...that she was...she was dead."

"Anything else?" I ask.

"Well, the police came with the ambulance, and then some important police boss arrived. His name was Elliott something, I think. And then they took Mrs. Monahan away."

"What about the young man in the black suit?" Burke asks.

"I guess that he left with them. I assumed he was Mrs. Monahan's assistant or her driver," says Cory Lawrence.

"Did you really *assume* that?" I ask with a tiny smirk.

"I always assume that," says Cory Lawrence.

"You are a wise young man, Mr. Lawrence. In a decade or so you will be running this store."

"Thank you, sir."

"But for the time being…Don't look now, but I would discreetly direct your eyes to the woman seated approximately ten yards to your left. She is wearing white slacks and a black silk shirt. You will notice that she has slipped on a brand new pair of Isabel Marant ankle boots, replacing them in the box with her scuffed and worn-out Blahnik pumps. *Merci et au revoir, Monsieur Lawrence.*"

CHAPTER 10

AN HOUR LATER DETECTIVE Burke and I walk into the art deco splendor of Eleven Madison Park.

"My God," says Burke. "I feel like I'm in an old black-and-white musical."

Suddenly, Marcella, the tall, thin, copper-haired beauty from the front desk, walks quickly toward me with her arms extended. Her smile is huge.

"Oh, here we go," says Burke.

She and I embrace.

"Luc, you're back. It's been at least a month," she says, shaking her hair. "Let me check on your table," she adds. "Have a flute of champagne while you're waiting. It's on the house, of course."

"*Merci,*" I say.

As the lovely Marcella walks away, Burke says, "*Merci,* my foot! What's going on, Moncrief? She's checking a table? We're on the job."

"But if the job takes place in one of New York's finest restaurants, it would actually be foolish not to partake of lunch."

"No. It would actually be foolish if we *were* to partake of lunch. About as unprofessional as you can get."

"Oh, K. Burke. You know I can always be much more unprofessional than this."

Needless to say, Burke does not laugh. She also refuses to join me in a glass of champagne. So we stand and wait in angry silence.

A few minutes later we are seated at a corner table.

"I'm not going to eat," says Burke.

"Didn't we have this identical conversation just last week?" I ask. As soon as I finish asking that question, a handsome fifty-ish man with close-cropped gray hair approaches the table.

"Mr. Moncrief, a pleasure, as always."

"This is my colleague, Detective Burke," I say. "This is the restaurant's manager, Paul deBarros."

As K. Burke gives a quick cold nod, deBarros pulls out a chair from the table and sits down.

Burke looks surprised, until I explain that deBarros witnessed the death of Jenna Lee Austin.

"Mrs. Austin was here at least once a week for lunch, and often for dinner," says the manager.

Burke and I follow the training rule: when the witness starts talking, do not interrupt. Let him get going. Sit back and listen.

"Sometimes Mrs. Austin dined with her husband. Sometimes she was with her mother. But the unfortunate day she died, she was dining alone. She told the front desk—Marcella was on that day—that perhaps she would be joined for coffee. She was not sure."

DeBarros takes a deep breath and shrugs his shoulders.

"Honestly, there's not much more to say. I welcomed her. I asked after her health. I asked after Mr. Austin. She was, as always, very bubbly and happy. I asked if she'd like something to drink before she ordered. She said she'd like a glass of San Pellegrino. A minute later, when I delivered it, she looked up at me. Then her head crashed onto the table."

"Who else saw this happen?" Burke asks.

"I'm not sure anyone else saw Mrs. Austin pass out. But when her head hit the table I shouted for help. So, of course, other diners looked, but it was early in the luncheon service, only a bit before noon. So there were not that many people here."

DeBarros describes how Jenna Austin was unresponsive to anything, although he admits that he did not follow the 911 operator's explicit instructions not to move her.

"I did not want to cause a disturbance for the other diners. So we carried Mrs. Austin to the passageway between the kitchen and the dining room. I'm certain she did not want people to see her in that condition."

"In *that* condition?" I ask. "Did you think she was drunk?"

"Oh, but of course not," he says. "I did not think she would want to be seen unconscious."

"Anything else, Detective?" I ask Burke. "The police? The ambulance?"

"Yes, all that. They gave her oxygen, I think, but the EMT said she was dead. I think they took her to Beth Israel hospital."

"Actually, it was NYU," Burke says.

"Thank you, Paul," I say. Burke thanks him also.

The captain rises from his seat. He gently pushes the chair back into place.

"Now, to travel from something tragic to something peaceful… if indeed you have no further questions…"

I have no further questions. The pattern is emerging, and that pattern is simple: no clue from any eyewitnesses. We will have to make sense of the boyfriend angle.

I ask K. Burke if she wants to ask anything. She shakes her head.

"In that case, Miss Burke, Mr. Moncrief, I have ordered a simple but interesting luncheon. To start with, a refreshing lobster ceviche with watermelon and lime ice. Then, if you agree, a Muscovy duck breast with lavender honey."

"Sounds wonderful," I say.

"Just coffee for me," says Burke.

"Bring Detective Burke the lobster ceviche. She may change her mind."

As soon as deBarros leaves, Burke hisses at me, "No. I told you I'm not doing this. I'm not eating. This is outrageous."

A few minutes later, after I've selected a Hugel Riesling as our wine, the lobster ceviche appears.

It is my pleasure to inform you that K. Burke ate every bit of it.

CHAPTER 11

ABOUT FIVE SECONDS AFTER Dalia died, I was certain of only one thing—that life was truly not worth living.

Yet everything else around me remained the same. People clogged the subways at rush hour. The *Mona Lisa* still smiled at the Louvre. Washington still crossed the Delaware at the Met. I was rich enough and skinny enough to wear the idiotic Milan fashion show suits, but I could bring myself to wear only Levi's and black T-shirts. People made love. People made war. I did neither.

Although I did not eat much, I made dinner reservations. I scheduled sessions with my personal trainer. And when my impeccably restored '65 Mustang needed work, I drove it to the mechanic in Yonkers who loved the car like a man loves his child.

I did go back to work, and that—along with my friendship with K. Burke—kept me from leaping from the rooftops.

I did make one big change, however. I never returned to the apartment I had shared with Dalia. I could not go back.

I lived briefly at the St. Regis Hotel. It was pleasant, and midtown Manhattan was certainly convenient. Hotel services made life easy—clean, crisp sheets every day, 4 a.m. room service deliveries of Caesar salads and Opus One wine. But after K. Burke persisted in jokingly calling me a "rich vagabond," I did as she suggested. I purchased a new apartment. A temple of simple luxury—cement flooring, spacious uncluttered walls, an occasional piece of iron or copper or steel furniture.

I return here this evening. After a day of investigation at Saks and Eleven Madison Park, I should be invigorated. Case work is my joy in life. Instead, the inevitable gloom of loneliness passes over me. I knew if I returned to our old apartment, I would never stop expecting to hear Dalia's voice from another room, to see her coat and scarf and pocketbook on the hallway chair, to hear her sound system blasting Selena Gomez. I wish. I wish I could hear her playing that obnoxious music again. I wish I could yell, "Turn off that crap!" I wish.

I do what I always do when I first arrive home from work, whether it is early in the evening or five in the morning. I take a shower—piercingly hot, Kiehl's coriander body wash, rinse with icy cold water. I step into sweat shorts and walk into the kitchen.

Lunch at Eleven Madison Park with K. Burke was delicious (and yes, I admit that we shared the orange chocolate bonbon for dessert), but it was a long time ago, so now I crack three eggs into a bowl. I whisk with a fork. Then I move to the eight-burner Wolf oven. (No, I did not forget the salt; Dalia was trying to make me cut down.) I melt a big knob of (unsalted) butter until it bubbles from the heat. I am about to pour the mixture into a pan when an echo-like disembodied voice fills the air. I know it well. The phone message machine is programmed to speak to me twenty minutes after I turn off the entrance door security alarm.

"You have two new messages," announces the small silver box on the kitchen island. Two? I seldom share my landline phone number, so there are usually *no* messages. Tonight there are *two*.

The first message promises to be a long, boring, and complicated piece of information from one of my late father's accountants. Something to do with German bonds and electronic stock certificates. I know that the accountant will call back. I move to the silver box and click Next.

The second message is a potentially important one.

"Mon cher enfant." My dear boy…with those three words I recognize the voice of Nicolas Savatier. He continues in French: "We have just arrived in Baltimore…preparing for the Preakness Stakes.…It would be most helpful if you could get in touch with us soon, very soon. We are heading to the Four Seasons on the harbor, where we are staying, but we always have our cell phones at hand. Please, if you would call soon."

In the background I hear Marguerite Savatier speaking loudly, *"Immédiatement."*

Then, from Nicolas, another *"immédiatement"* followed by a soft and courteous *"Merci."*

I return the call *immédiatement*.

CHAPTER 12

"*MON CHER LUC,* WE did not want to alarm you," says Nicolas, ever the perfect French gentleman.

"Give me the phone, Nicolas," I hear Marguerite say, in French. Then I hear her voice clearly on the phone.

"Luc. It is you?"

"*Mais oui,*" I say. "What is the problem?"

We both switch to French.

"We are not quite certain that it is an actual problem. And, of course, we do not want to alarm you…"

"Or trouble you," comes the voice of Nicolas, now relegated to the background.

"Please," I almost shout. "You are *not* alarming me. You are *not* troubling me. What is the matter? Speak, please, speak."

Marguerite continues.

"Perhaps it is not worth getting excited about," she says.

I am thinking that if they were with me in person I would wring their aristocratic necks, or at least toss a glass of Veuve Clicquot in their faces. Finally, Marguerite speaks. Her voice is trembling:

"I have received two dozen red roses," Marguerite says. "A deliveryman was waiting with them when we landed in Baltimore."

I, of course, instinctively know that there is more to this phone call, that not everything has been revealed. Even a slightly dotty elderly couple would not become frightened by a box of flowers. However, I proceed as if all will turn out normally.

"How delightful. Who sent the roses?" I ask.

"We do not know," Marguerite says. "It is anonymous. And *c'est ça le problème.*"

Suddenly, Nicolas's voice is on the phone.

"You see, the greater problem is that, yes, it is unsigned, *but* there *is* a note with the roses. Let me read it to you."

Nicolas's frail voice becomes strong: "'Win the Preakness. Or you will suffer the consequences.'"

I keep my own voice calm, but this is surely not the sort of note anyone wishes to receive.

"Did you try contacting the florist?" I ask. (Yes, I know, a foolish and obvious question.)

"*Encore une fois, mon cher Luc.* We may be old but we are not stupid," says Nicolas. "There was no name on the card or on the box. We signed for them without thinking, figuring it was just more congratulatory flowers. It wasn't until we were in the cab that we even thought to look at the card. It is so mysterious."

I am thinking that it is not just mysterious, but it is so creepy, really creepy. Is it a threat? A joke? A mistake?

To put the Savatiers at ease I say something that I don't fully believe. "This is nothing to be alarmed about."

Then I quickly add, "Listen. The Preakness is next Saturday. I've got work to do up here. But if you need me, I'll drop everything and join you. Okay?"

"Okay," says Nicolas.

In the background, just before I hang up, I hear Marguerite's voice in a loud stage whisper: "Tell him to come down now."

Click.

The butter for the eggs is now burnt to a foul brown grease, and the smoke detector is screaming at me. So my dinner becomes a bowl of Special K and two large glasses of Bouchard Montrachet.

I don't sleep. Not a wink. My bedtime companion is the relentless stream of grim BBC detective shows and one more glass of the soft chardonnay. Between the ending of *Wallander* and the start of *Vera* comes dawn.

CHAPTER 13

Mara Monahan
2 East 79th Street

TODAY BURKE AND I visit the Manhattan apartments of the three beautiful murder victims. Burke has made some interesting connections in the three cases: Each one of the murdered women was, of course, beautiful and wealthy. But there's something more. Each of them had an only child below the age of three. All these rich women, of course, also had household help—maids, drivers, housemen, housekeepers, cooks, nannies. It's the nannies who interest Burke and me. In reading the reports, Burke noticed that all three of the nannies were placed by the same employment agency in London. Funny. In detective work you have to be very careful of coincidences, and then again, you can't be *too* careful.

An attractive, excessively energetic young woman with a demure hairstyle opens the door of the Monahan apartment.

The young woman wants to appear properly somber, but she cannot hide the sometimes chronic American characteristic of perkiness.

"I'm Congressman Monahan's District Assistant, Chloe Garrison," she says. "Please come in." We walk into a big foyer with traditional Upper East Side black-and-white tiled marble floors.

"The congressman wanted to be here himself to speak with

you," she says, then quickly adds, "But he was on the first flight down to DC today. There's an environmental waste bill in debate…and…well, he thought it would be most helpful if he got back to work." We agree again.

"NYPD has already spoken to Mr. Monahan," Burke says. "He's been very cooperative…especially given the painfulness of the situation."

Chloe nods. "Congressman Monahan is taking Henry, their little boy, out to Montauk this weekend. Like you said, the whole death thing is pretty…tough."

"No doubt about it," Burke says.

The assistant grants our request to speak to Henry's nanny, Mrs. Meade-Grafton. "If it's all right, you'll meet in Congressman Monahan's home office."

The home office has a spectacular view of Central Park, and Mrs. Meade-Grafton does not remotely look like what I thought a British nanny named "Mrs. Meade-Grafton" would. She is wearing stretch jeans that cling quite snuggly to her ample hips and thighs. She sits on a black leather sofa, and her legs are tucked beneath her. Her white T-shirt has these words printed on the front:

I LISTEN TO BANDS THAT DON'T EXIST YET.

We introduce ourselves. Mrs. Meade-Grafton does not stand to greet us, but she does extend her very fleshy hand. The congressional aide leaves the room.

"Is young Henry around?" Burke asks.

"Oh, the little one is watchin' telly. Cook's keepin' an eye on 'im," the nanny says. English is definitely *my* second language, but you don't have to be 'enry 'iggins to know that it is a fairly lower-class accent.

I ask how she and the late Mrs. Monahan got along.

"Like two peas," she says. "An' why not? We didn't see very much of one 'nother. I was with little 'enry when she wasn't. And when she was seein' to the little lad then myself mostly wasn't there. But Mrs. M was a decent enough sort. Quite a loss, o' course. Not sure the 'usband 'as took it all in yet. An' to be honest, little 'enry might be thinkin' his mum's still just out shoppin'."

She laughs. A lot.

CHAPTER 14

Jenna Lee Austin
156 Perry Street

JULIA HIGHRIDGE PREFERS TO be called *Miss* Highridge, *and* she prefers to be called a governess, not a nanny. Wardrobe? A dark plaid tweed suit, sensible shoes, hair in a bun. Miss Highridge is probably forty years old, but with her grooming and wardrobe she could pass for fifty. She is as formal as Mrs. Meade-Grafton was informal.

We sit in the first floor Victorian parlor of an impeccably decorated Greenwich Village townhouse. We are only a block from the West Side Highway, the Hudson River just on the other side of that.

"So, you look after Ethan?" Burke asks.

"That would be *Master* Ethan. And yes, Master Ethan is my charge."

Then she gestures to a small table. On the table is a silver tray covered with a silver teapot, teacups, a large plate of cookies, and various pastries.

"I thought you might need some tea. I've also had the cook bring in some puddings and cakes. You may not be familiar with all of them, these especially…"

"I am happy to tell you that I am completely familiar with these. They are *canelés,* and I have not seen them ever before here in New York," I say. *"Je les adore."* I adore them. "They are my favorite."

I am not merely being a polite guest. I am telling the truth about the crunchy little dome-like butter pastries that are in every patisserie in Paris. I've not found any that taste as good as they do there. And believe me, I've tried every one in New York.

"Ah," Miss Highridge says. "An authentic Frenchman. Perhaps you would like to conduct the interview in French. I'm fluent."

"No," I say. "I think English is the more appropriate language for an NYPD investigation. Plus, my colleague might not…"

Burke interrupts. She is not at all amused. "Have a canelé, Detective Moncrief. And let's get on with it."

Miss Highridge goes on to tell us that she was enormously fond of Mrs. Lenz—"That would be *Mrs.* Austin to you."

Burke, losing none of her edge, says, "We know her husband is Bernard Lenz. He's been interviewed twice already."

We ask for her opinion of Jenna Lee Austin.

Her answer: "She was an actress. That should tell you everything." Then she proceeds to pop a third canelé into her mouth.

"That really does *not* tell us very much, Miss Highridge," I say.

"Then let me explain. She knew how to *act* like a mother. Just as she knew how to *act* like a good wife. But…please, have another cake…"

Both Burke and I decline.

"In any event, I suppose she wanted to be a good mother. But her career came first. She cared so very much about her career. The lessons, and the private trainer and the yoga instructor and the homeopathic doctor and the nutritionist and…oh, so many people to help her. But Mr. Lenz didn't seem to mind."

Miss Highridge pauses, pops another pastry, then speaks: "Her husband had *his* life. She had *hers*. And Master Ethan had *me*."

We talk some more. Miss Highridge says that Jenna Lee seemed to have a lot of friends.

"How about her marriage?"

"The marriage was what most marriages are. A series of small compromises."

When we are ready to leave, she agrees to get in touch if she thinks of anything helpful. But, she tells us, "That seems unlikely."

Then she says, "Let me have these extra canelés wrapped for you. You can take them with you."

"*Non merci, mademoiselle.* You enjoy them."

"Oh, dear. It's the last thing I need," she says. She pats her significantly round belly, and we escape without the little cakes.

CHAPTER 15

Tessa Fulbright
River House, 435 East 52nd Street

MAZIE McCRAY LOVED TESSA Fulbright. My instincts tell me that immediately.

"First I raised her mother, Mrs. Pierce. Then I raised Tessa…I mean, of course, Mrs. Fulbright. And now my last job will be raising Andrew. But I never expected not having his mother by my side while doing it."

Mazie dabs at her eyes with a crumbled tissue. Mazie is black and round and perfectly charming. Mazie, Burke, and I are sitting on low children-sized benches in Andrew's bright-yellow nursery. Andrew toddles around, chubby arms extended. He falls. He giggles. He laughs. He gets up and walks some more.

Suddenly Mazie stands up and walks quickly to Andrew. Mazie lifts the child. He rests in Mazie's arms, and Mazie uses her free hands to cover the boy's ears.

"Tessa, Andrew's mother, was fine, absolutely fine, a wonderful child, a wonderful woman. Then she married Mr. Fulbright. Then she started in with 'I'm not pretty enough. I'm not young enough.'" Mazie shakes her head thoughtfully, and then fixes her eyes on Burke and me.

"You two saw her," she says. "You must've seen photos. She was beautiful. The most beautiful woman. Even more important, she was a *good* woman. I knew her. I raised her. I knew her better than anyone."

A long pause. Then K. Burke speaks softly.

"What do you think happened?"

Mazie places Andrew back on the floor. The little boy returns to his giddy, happy walking. Mazie takes a deep breath, shakes her head, and speaks.

"I wish I knew. Dear Lord, I just wish I knew."

CHAPTER 16

I SLEEP WELL. BUT don't assume that sleep comes to me easily. No, not at all. My sleep is a chemical and musical trick. It requires 10mg of Ambien, followed a half hour later by 5mg of Xanax, and then I queue up the Luc Moncrief Artist of the Week on the sound system. This can be anything from Chopin to the Rolling Stones. This week, I'm sleeping with the little-known Vienna Teng. Her music is just slow enough to lullaby me a bit, just fast enough to let me know I'm still breathing.

Sleep arrives suddenly. And just as suddenly I am awake. The telephone is ringing. It is morning. The big bedroom is filled with soft morning light.

I grab the receiver.

"Yes, what is it?"

"Luc? It is so early," comes the old woman's voice. I recognize it immediately.

"Marguerite, what's wrong?" I say.

My neck hurts. My lips are dry. An Ambien-induced sleep brings sleep, but it rarely brings peace.

"Many things. I'll put Nicolas on."

"The news is bad," he says.

I can only imagine. And I want to know everything right this moment. I do not want the Servatiers to begin dithering.

"Stop! Do not tell me anything except what the goddamn problem is," I say. I have purposely chosen the curse word to demonstrate my seriousness.

"It is a murder," the old man shouts back at me.

"A murder. A murder of whom? Tell me. Keep talking."

I don't understand what he's saying at first…then I deduce a horse has been killed.

"Which horse?" I ask. Nicolas says something I don't understand in half-French, half-English.

"Say it again, sir. Say the horse's name again." I hear something like "Charlene Bay."

"Charlene Bay?" I ask, just one impatient step away from a shout.

"No. Not Charlene," he says.

"A bay? The horse is a bay?"

"Luc. You are not listening properly," Nicolas says.

I restrain myself from becoming angry at the anxious old man.

"Speak slower…slower and louder," I say.

He says the name again. Slower and louder.

This time I get it. "Charlie-Boy? The horse's name is Charlie-Boy?" I ask.

"*Ah, oui. Son nom est Shar-lee-Boy.* Charlie-Boy."

He continues.

"The security people say they heard a noise. They go into the stable, and there he lay. His throat was sliced, they think, with the electrical saw, the machine a man uses to cut down a tree. It made me sick. Marguerite wept."

My response is "Holy shit!"

Nicolas has yet more information.

"Charlie-Boy was the Pimlico exercise horse. The warm-ups. As you know, the warm-ups are so important."

I remember. Only a few days ago Nicolas described the important job of the warm-up horse to K. Burke and me. But the lesson here, in the most graphic terms possible, was: Do as I say, or Garçon is next.

As I am recalling that excellent lesson, Nicolas passes the phone to his wife.

"What should we do?" says Marguerite.

I am, of course, thinking of the note the Savatiers received. *Win the Preakness. Or you will suffer the consequences.*

There is just one thing to do. I tell them what they want to hear.

"I have to come down there immediately," I say.

She conveys this news to Nicolas. I can hear him talking loudly in the background.

"No, Luc. We do not want to be a bother. We only…"

"*Au revoir, mes amis.* I'll see you both soon."

"But Luc…" I hear Marguerite, and I am forced to be an American.

"Gotta go, guys." Click.

CHAPTER 17

WE WALK TOWARD STABLE A-2 at Pimlico Race Course.

It is almost noon on Wednesday. The sky is clear. The temperature is seventy-six degrees.

"I wish we could bottle this weather and save it for next Saturday's race," says Detective Kwame Clarke of the Baltimore Police Department.

I am walking with Detective Clarke, Marguerite and Nicolas Savatier, two Pimlico officials, and Nina Helstein. Miss Helstein is an investigating officer from TOBA, the Thoroughbred Owners and Breeders Association. They have kept the scene intact for us.

We walk, almost like people in a funeral procession, into the stable.

We stare down at the lifeless body of Charlie-Boy.

My father raised horses at his home in Avignon, but they never particularly interested me (especially since Avignon was only a two-hour drive to the beaches of Nice, with their beautiful waters and topless women).

Perhaps because I have spent so little time with horses, whenever I see these animals I am always surprised that they are so big.

This dead horse, Charlie-Boy, looks…well…gigantic. A huge

dead pile of tremendous muscles, a heap of giant thighs and legs and torso. Yards of white linen bandages are tied tightly around Charlie-Boy's massive neck. The bandages are splotched with red blood. Bloody hay is scattered around the horse's neck and head. The straw is also caked with blood.

Marguerite looks down at the floor. Nicolas looks up toward the wooden rafters. After what feels like an appropriate amount of time, Detective Clarke speaks quietly to me.

"There's a trainers' lounge in Stable A-4. I'll wait for you there. Say, in about ten minutes."

I nod yes, and then I walk with the Savatiers to another stable, the stable where Garçon is being kept. Both Marguerite and Nicolas break into sobs when they see their horse. Armand Joscoe, Garçon's jockey, smiles gently. Joscoe and a tall young man are methodically stroking Garçon's neck and back.

"Ah, Monsieur Moncrief," says Armand. *"Une véritable tragédie."*

The young man with Joscoe addresses me: *"Bonjour, Monsieur Moncrief."*

I have no idea who this teenager is. Then Armand Joscoe tells me in French that "Perhaps you remember Léon, my little boy. He is all grown up."

"He certainly is," I say. I am amazed Léon has become a veritable six-footer. He is quite handsome, freshly showered, and I can't help but notice that he is impeccably dressed. I also can't help but notice how expensive his clothing is. He looks more like one of the well-heeled spectators than his hard-working father.

The Joscoe men and I all smile at the different heights of father and son, but our smiles do not come from the heart. It is impossible. The stable is too filled with sadness and fear.

Here, the second step on the way to the Triple Crown, a wonderful horse with wonderful owners, an occasion that should be so festive. Now it is all so terribly grim.

A few minutes later I walk into a room attached to Stable A-4. The room is small, with two worn leather sofas, a stack of dirty, smelly jodhpurs in one corner, a soda machine in another corner.

Detective Clarke smiles when I enter.

"You were probably expecting something a bit fancier for Pimlico," he says.

"I never expect anything," I say. "That way I'm never disappointed."

"That's a perfect New York philosophy," says Clarke.

"It is also a French philosophy, I think."

Clarke is a small man, black, and completely bald. He also wears a suit (I can't help myself from comment here) whose cut and quality seem quite elegant for what I know a detective's pay level to be, especially in Kentucky. In any event, he is smart, and he is extremely likable.

"Your friends have filled me in," he says. "And Miss Helstein is talking to yet more of the track officials."

"The Savatiers are terribly frightened," I say.

"With good cause," he says.

He hands me a neatly folded letter-sized piece of paper. I open it and see that it is a copy of the threatening note that was sent to the Savatiers.

Win the Preakness. Or you will suffer the consequences.

"What do you think?" I ask.

"I think that it is very much what it appears to be—a scary, gruesome, inscrutable threat. I really wish you or the Savatiers had contacted me earlier…"

"They only told me about it yesterday."

"Doesn't matter. Anyway, I sent the original note to the lab. Frankly, I don't think they'll come up with anything. Prints and stuff like that only happen on TV. All we can do is keep watching Pimlico, up and down, east to west."

"Any other suggestions?" I say.

"Well, I would strongly suggest they try to persuade their horse to win the race on Saturday."

"I wish I had thought of that," I say.

Kwame Clarke laughs. We both give very weak smiles. Then Clarke says, "My instincts tell me that the horse-murder and the threatening note are *not* connected. I've got absolutely no proof. But I just feel that if there was a connection we'd see it. The whole thing is just a little too baroque, bizarre. You know what I mean?"

Another detective with *instinct*. I knew I liked this guy.

"My instinct's the same as yours," I say. Then I add, "Two cops with the same unsubstantiated idea. We must be wrong, huh?"

We're in no mood to laugh. I speak.

"Look, my friends are scared. And I don't blame them."

"I don't, either. We've put three plainclothes people—two men, one woman—around the stables. We've got three other detectives checking everyone and everything coming in—florists, caterers, workers, set-up people, tent people."

"How about you assign some protection for my friends?"

"Detective, I don't know about the NYPD, but here in Baltimore there's always a shortage in manpower. I can't loosen one or two people for a civilian guard."

"Let me ask this. Do you have anyone who's looking for some freelance work on their days off?"

"Plenty of those, but like I just said, there's no budget for it."

"Do me a favor, if you don't mind. Get three people to follow the Savatiers. I'll feel a whole lot better. And I'll come up with the cash. I'm going to be back down here next Friday night for the race on Saturday. I'll give you cash to pay your guys."

Clarke does a goofy over-the-top double-take.

"Way to go, New York!" he shouts.

Kwame Clarke throws his right hand up into the air. *Shit.* I must try to execute a high-five, always a disaster for me. We complete the gesture clumsily (on my end, at least), and almost immediately my cell phone rings.

Of course, I know who it is, and I know what the greeting will be. I click on the phone.

"Where the hell are you, Moncrief?"

I answer the question.

"And good day to you also. I'm afraid, K. Burke, that our work has followed us to the races."

CHAPTER 18

AFTER MY PLANE TAKES off from Baltimore's Thurgood Marshall Airport we receive information that travel from our reserved airport, White Plains, into Manhattan is a mess. I don't know how my pilot does it, but he manages to get last-minute clearance at LaGuardia.

I walk through the private aircraft gate and immediately hear a shout.

"Moncrief! Over here!"

It can only be K. Burke.

"I've got a patrol car and driver outside. We've got to get our butts over to Central Park West. We can catch up on the way," she says. I follow her quick step toward the exit.

Instead of asking why "our butts" are so urgently required on Central Park West, I ask, "How did you know I'd be here, at *this* airport?"

"I have top-secret access to a special communication device. It's called a telephone. I used it to track you down."

I stop myself from saying that I thought perhaps she had the powers of a gypsy woman. Instead I simply say, "Ingenious, K. Burke. You should become a detective."

"And right now you should become familiar with what's going on at 145 Central Park West. It seems…"

The police siren blares as our car enters the expressway.

"One-forty-five?" I say. "That's the San Remo. 74th Street. *Très élégant;* I have a good friend who lives there…"

"Why am I not surprised?" Burke says. "Who?"

"Juan Carlos Vilca, the Peruvian polo player, and his wife, Gabriela," I say. "She's a professional model. She is exquisite."

"Do you know anyone who isn't exquisite?" A quick pause, then she says, "Wait. Don't answer that. I just thought of someone who isn't. And you're sitting next to her."

"That is *your* opinion, K. Burke," I say. That conversation goes no further. She moves on.

"Meanwhile, there are a few facts you should know about a dead neighbor of your Peruvian friends."

Burke tells me that at two o'clock this afternoon a personal assistant to a rich young woman by the name of Elspeth Tweddle found her dead in her bedroom.

"Tweddle?" I ask. "That is a real name? It sounds like the name of a talking duck in a child's storybook."

"Elspeth Tweddle is a very real name, and Elspeth Tweddle is a very dead woman. And, there's a bit of background information. She's twenty-five years old. And take a look. As you would say, truly exquisite."

K. Burke clicks a photo of Elspeth Tweddle on her iPad. The woman may be twenty-five, but she could pass for eighteen.

This woman *is* exquisite, truly beautiful. A big pouty look on her face, with light-green eyes, and chestnut hair with the fashionable blond streaks.

Burke tells me that they are called champagne streaks.

"When the streaks have more gold in them than blond," she explains, "the color is called champagne.'"

"I love to learn, K. Burke. And that is good, because you love to teach."

Burke ignores me. Then she tells me more about the woman with the champagne streaks.

The woman's personal assistant came in at two. He usually arrived at ten, but the woman had a dentist appointment and he had arranged to not arrive until after lunch.

"The assistant found her sprawled on the floor, and since Tweddle was rich and beautiful, 911 actually remembered to call us. She was dead when the ME got there."

At this moment our squad car pulls up to the first of the two San Remo apartment towers. The doorman opens the car door.

"Good morning, Mr. Moncrief. Is Mr. Vilca expecting you?" he asks.

"No, Ernie. I am here today on official business."

K. Burke takes charge. "I'm Detective Burke, and apparently you already know Detective Moncrief. We will be joining a few other members of the NYPD on the…"

Ernie finishes her sentence. "The twelfth floor. There are quite a few people up there already. Take a left at the end of this hall, and that'll be your elevator."

As we wait for the elevator I ask Burke, "So, what are you thinking? Do we know if this case fits the same pattern as the other three?"

"The only thing that fits is that the victim or the 'dead woman,' if you prefer, is very pretty, very young, and very rich. There the similarities end. Miss Tweddle is *not* married. Miss Tweddle does *not* have children. And so Miss Tweddle does *not* have an overweight nanny."

"Hmmm. Yet it *feels…it feels…*" I begin to say. Burke holds her hand up like a traffic cop. She speaks.

"I'm with you. It sure as hell smells like the other three deaths."

"Mademoiselle Tweddle lives alone?"

Burke looks down at her notes.

"Well, there's a live-in cook, a live-in maid, and another maid who doesn't live there. Miss Tweddle's personal assistant comes in five days a week. But there are a few other things I've got to tell you…"

Then the elevator arrives. The elevator man pulls wide the bronze gates, and two young boys wearing blue blazers and gray flannel slacks get off the elevator.

Burke and I ride up to the twelfth floor in silence. She's not about to tell me anything in front of the elevator man.

We finally arrive on twelve. Two police officers nod and gesture toward the open apartment door. But Burke pauses before we enter.

"Let me finish the background," she says. "Elspeth Tweddle lives here, but this is her mother's apartment. The victim grew up in this apartment. Elspeth never moved out."

"The mother is deceased?"

"No, she's very much alive. Elspeth's mother, Rose Jensen Tweddle, is currently the American ambassador to Italy."

CHAPTER 19

THE POLICE SCENE HAS not been touched. Pristine. Just the way we like it when we show up.

The victim is lying on her back on the bedroom floor. She wears only a sports bra and cut-off gray sweatpants.

Jonny Liang, the assistant medical examiner, approaches us immediately. Jonny handled Tessa Fulbright's case.

"A quick on-site blood test is telling us no drug abuse, but we won't know for sure until we get the full autopsy going," Jonny says.

Jonny's a smart guy. Before Burke or I can say a word, he anticipates our next question.

"I know. From a circumstantial point of view, it looks just like your other three 'rich gal' cases. Yet so far the forensics don't support that conclusion. Wait until tonight or tomorrow morning. I'll get you the information fast."

"Assuming there *is* information," Burke says. I share her skepticism, but something is bugging me. Before I can even think about what that nagging feeling might be, a handsome young blond man—no more than thirty years old—approaches us.

"Good morning, detectives. I'm Ian Hart. I'm Miss Tweddle's personal assistant."

"I'm happy to tell you what I told the police officers," Hart says. My instinct is that this guy is a sleazebag—too handsome for his own good. I notice his four-hundred-dollar jeans, and consider that he spends each day with the ambassador's beautiful daughter.

I immediately glance at the bed and consider if more than one person has been in it. No. Just one side of the king-size bed looks slept in.

But I rethink that instinct as he speaks. This guy comes across as smart and strong. He's also somber, like a guy who is authentically sad that he's lost a friend.

For the most part I learn nothing that I haven't already heard from K. Burke. He does, however, point to a small desk near the window. On that desk is a coffee mug with the initials "ET" on it.

"She had a lot of ET stuff," Hart says. "Her initials, you know."

Burke nods. She obviously figured that out. Elspeth Tweddle.

I also nod. I would never tell this to Burke, but I did not figure that out.

Burke tells one of the officers to "bag" the coffee mug contents and get it to the lab.

"What exactly were your responsibilities with Miss Tweddle?" I ask.

"The usual PA stuff—lunch reservations, dinner reservations, dealing with what little correspondence she had. But a lot of the things she did…well, we did together. We played squash. We went to parties together. We'd run in the park. We went riding in the park a lot. And she was working on this documentary. She had all these home videos of her and her family's summers on Fishers Island."

Clearly Ian Hart interprets our silence and our occasional nods as indication that we thought his boss's life—not to mention his own job—was pretty frivolous.

He says, "Listen. I know it kind of sounds like I was being paid to be Elspeth's friend. And in a way I was. But I really liked the days I spent with her. She was smart and she was pretty and she was fun."

He looks away from us. He blinks his eyes quickly. He looks back at us, composed. He smiles.

"She was my friend," he says.

Later, as we wait for the elevator, Burke says, "You know one of the toughest things in detective work?"

She does not wait for my answer. Instead she gives her own answer.

"It's whether grieving people are telling the truth. In those moments, I never quite know for sure when someone is bullshitting me—or even being honest with themselves."

"I am not so good at it myself," I say. We are silent for a few seconds.

Then Burke says, "So, they went riding a lot. You've got quite a few horses in your life these days, Moncrief."

As we walk from the elevator to the door I say to Burke, "*Alors.*

You have reminded me. You know that white dress in which you looked so magnificent at the Kentucky Derby?"

"What about that dress?" She asks the question suspiciously.

"Have it washed and ironed. Next Friday night we are leaving for Baltimore. The next day is…"

She knows. She yells, "The Preakness!"

CHAPTER 20

THE SAVATIERS' HORSE, GARÇON, came to Louisville as an anonymous foreigner. He comes to Baltimore as a worldwide celebrity, the favorite.

Garçon now has a really good shot at capturing the Triple Crown, the honor that goes to the rare horse who wins the Kentucky Derby, the Preakness Stakes, and the Belmont Stakes. This possibility is beyond thrilling—only twelve times, in over one hundred years of thoroughbred racing, has a horse won the Triple Crown.

Only a few days ago I was here to view the remains of a horse, a mysterious and disgusting slaughter. But we carry on. We have tried our best to tuck the event in the back of our brains. Even the ominous threats and flowers sent to the Savatiers cannot eradicate our nervous hopes. The Savatiers are worried, but they are certainly not defeated. The hired bodyguards and Detective Kwame Clarke have been staying very close to them.

Now, if only the weather would cooperate.

It is a miserable day. Cold rain everywhere. Umbrellas are everywhere. Serious raincoat weather. Pimlico Race Course is becoming Pimlico River.

K. Burke and I wait in the stable with the Savatiers. Wet hay sticks to our water-soaked shoes. Rain pelts the stable roof.

But Garçon's jockey, Armand Joscoe, keeps smiling and tells Burke and me not to worry. Then he gives us some information to keep us calm.

"Le cheval aime la boue," the little guy says.

"Très bien, Armand. Très bien." Then I turn to Burke and translate.

"The horse likes mud!" I say.

"Merci," Burke says. "And may I remind you for the hundredth time that I speak French." She speaks sweetly, but there is a touch of irritation in her voice.

"Where is your son, Armand?" I ask. He tells me that Léon is occupied elsewhere. But of course, he will be watching.

Burke speaks.

"Have you noticed, Moncrief, that you, me, Marguerite, and Nicolas are all wearing the same clothes we wore at the Derby?"

I look.

"Mon Dieu," I say. "Unbelievable." But it is not really unbelievable.

The four of us seem to be honoring a superstition: Everything must be as it was in Louisville. Marguerite is in her bright floral suit. Nicolas in his perfectly cut gray slacks and blue blazer. Katherine Burke in her white linen dress with the Savatiers' racing silk colors belted around her waist.

I move in close to K. Burke and whisper, "Do you think Madame Savatier is wearing the same undergarments as she did in Louisville?"

K. Burke looks away from me, as if I am a naughty-minded schoolboy and she is the little girl I chose to shock.

Then a tremendous blare of trumpets. The moment is upon us.

CHAPTER 21

THIRTY SECONDS LATER AN announcement comes from the loudspeakers: "Horses and jockeys will now proceed to the track!"

We walk a few yards with Armand Joscoe and Garçon. After a few minutes the horse and rider turn. They walk toward the water-drenched track, and the rest of us find our places in the owners' circle.

The parade is magnificent, a combination of beauty and strength. Marguerite is seated to my right. She holds my hand. Katherine Burke sits to my left. She holds a pair of high-powered binoculars. Me? I occasionally glance at the equine parade, but mostly I keep a keen eye on the many people seated near us. Who might be watching us? Who might want to harm the Savatiers?

I would like to report that the sun broke out before the race began. It did not. The rain keeps on raining, but it seems a little more cooperative. It seems to fall in a softer, more peaceful rhythm. We wait for the race to start.

I say, "You will recall, K. Burke, that during the plane ride down here you insisted that I was *not* to place a bet for you on Garçon?"

"Of course I do. It was just a sudden superstition on my part. I didn't think he'd win this time if we placed a bet."

"Well, I disobeyed and did so anyway," I say. "But I bet only a hundred dollars."

She's pissed. She turns away from me and mutters, "Damn it. Do you ever listen?"

I say nothing. So she speaks again.

"When I specifically asked you not to? It's bad karma, Moncrief. You're pushing your luck…my luck…our luck."

"But, K. Burke, we are trying to do everything in the same way as we did in Kentucky, *n'est-ce pas?*" I say.

"*N'est-ce pas,* my foot. I think it feels selfish to bet, to feel so smug about winning. If Garçon loses, I'm blaming it on you."

"We shall see. And please, not to worry. This time cannot be exactly like last time. At the Derby Garçon was a long shot. Today he is the favorite. Today his odds are a measly two-to-one. Even if he wins you will only…"

But my attention is suddenly elsewhere. A few yards away from K. Burke I see Detective Kwame Clarke taking a seat. Clarke watches us. Our eyes meet. He tips his umbrella handle in my direction. We both nod to one another.

Marguerite speaks to me.

"I am scared, Luc. Very scared," she says.

"There is no reason…"

"Yes. Yes. I know that you have the private guards watching us. And I know Detective Clarke is nearby. But I am nonetheless frightened."

"You have no need to be," I say. "All is secure."

But I am wise enough to know that, like me, Marguerite is thinking about that dark and threatening note.

Win the Preakness. Or you will suffer the consequences.

"What if Garçon does not win?" she says.

I don't have time to answer. We hear the sound of a bell. Marguerite grabs my hand.

The race begins.

CHAPTER 22

ARMAND JOSCOE, THE JOCKEY *extraordinaire,* turns out to be a psychic *extraordinaire.*

Joscoe's assurance that Garçon "likes mud" turns out to be absolutely true! It becomes clear in the first few moments of the race that Garçon doesn't merely *like* mud. Garçon *loves* mud! Physically, spiritually, indisputably. With mud painting his hooves and legs, Garçon does not merely gallop, he flies.

Yes, we remain nervous. We are still anxious. But it is so much better to be nervous and anxious with a winning horse.

But not only does he win, he wins *decisively.* We all go nuts, and for the second time in two weeks, we are celebrating like crazy people.

The Savatiers are ecstatic, but it is also clear to me that both of them are anxious. Marguerite's hands tremble. Her head keeps turning back and forth. Officials (including Kwame Clarke) arrive quickly to lead the couple to the presentation circle.

"My friends must come with us," Marguerite says to Detective Clarke.

"No, no," I say. "You will be well cared for, and Detective Burke and I will be standing nearby."

Burke leans into me.

"Moncrief, she's shaking. She's a nervous mess. What difference does it make? Let's go with them."

Burke's logic is impeccable, of course.

"Very well," I say. Marguerite Savatier turns to Burke: "*You, Mademoiselle Burke,* are a very fine influence on our Luc." Hmmm. I could swear there was a flash of romantic mischief in Marguerite's eyes.

So we join the owners. Then, a few moments later, the four of us join the triumphant horse and the smiling jockey. Garçon is covered in a huge blanket of yellow flowers.

"Those are Viking poms. They're meant to look like Black-Eyed Susans, the official state flower of Maryland," Burke says to me.

"Is there anything you do not know, K. Burke?" I ask.

"Well, I don't know how much money we won on that race," she says with a twinkle in her eye. Then we both turn our attention to the trophy presentation, as well as the presentation of a large bouquet of Black-Eyed Susans to Madame Savatier. The old woman smiles for the cameras. Applause. Smiles. The thousands of click-click-click from cameras.

I feel a buzz from my cell phone. I try looking at the screen as discreetly as possible. A message from Inspector Elliott.

Where the hell r u 2?

I text back. See u soon.

He texts back. WTF?

I slip the phone back into my pocket.

The speeches from corporate sponsors and the governor of Maryland are mercifully short. Then we stand at attention—for the third time—and listen to yet another rendition of "Maryland, My Maryland."

CHAPTER 23

THE MOMENT BURKE AND I break from our group and head to the after-party she says, "That message you got was from Elliott, wasn't it?"

"Indeed it was. He asked about our whereabouts. I told him that we would be in touch soon. Not to worry," I say.

"We should get back up to New York now," she says.

"In due time, K. Burke. For the moment, a celebration."

The party in the Pimlico Club room is lavish, even more so than the post-race party in Louisville. Instead of mint juleps, Pimlico serves a cocktail called the Black-Eyed Susan.

"I think they put every fruit juice in the world in this drink," says K. Burke.

I ask a nearby waiter what goes into this concoction. He practically quotes Burke: "Any fruit juice you can name—orange, pineapple, lime. Then a lot of vodka and a little bourbon."

Burke and I each put down a few drinks. Indeed, will Burke and I ever find a race-party cocktail that we do *not* like?

It should be a festive day. Garçon has won. The party is noisy and happy and fun. Instead of Louisville's tiny hush puppy hors d'oeuvres, we are served miniature crab cakes. The crowd is elegant. The music is loud. The DJ plays Randy Newman and Bruce Springsteen and Lyle Lovett and even Counting Crows. And every song is—amazingly—a song about Baltimore.

I pull out my phone and pull up my favorite horse-racing blog. I have to yell to be heard over the music and celebration, but I read this part to K. Burke:

"As a Frenchman loves champagne, so does Preakness favorite Vilain Garçon love mud. Yes, Vilain Garçon easily grabbed hold of step two in his bid for the Triple Crown. This extraordinary steed, owned by a charming elderly French couple, Marguerite and Nicolas (no "h," *s'il vous plait*), and ridden by the until-now unknown jockey, Armand Joscoe, won the Preakness decisively this afternoon. Not by a nose, but by a full length. The rain-drenched crowd is reacting with wild shouts. As for this reporter, I will suggest to the Savatiers that, when the Belmont Stakes comes along, that they pray for rain. If their prayers are answered, then the Triple Crown is certain."

Burke pretends to listen, but she's chewing on the orange peel from her cocktail. As always, however, she is on the job.

"Shall we check in with your buddy Kwame and the Baltimore PD?" she asks.

"Certainly. If you ever finish your orange peel," I say. She makes a face and puts the peel back in the glass. Then we both walk to the entrance archway where Kwame Clarke and two men in gray suits are standing, bodyguards for the Savatiers. The cut of their boxy suits immediately tells me that these are two officers.

Introductions all around.

"Aha, now I finally meet the extraordinary K. Burke," says Kwame Clarke.

Burke nods her head in my direction and says to Clarke, "You didn't hear that word 'extraordinary' about me from Moncrief, I'm sure."

Smiles all around.

K. Burke and Kwame Clarke shake hands. Perhaps an usually long handshake, I think.

It occurs to me that Burke and Clarke have noticed…how to put this?…how good-looking the other is.

Why does this annoy me?

Clarke introduces me to the officers—Vinnie Masucci and Olan Washington. They explain that they are eyeballing everybody who comes in.

"If the name's not on the invite list, they're not at the party," says Masucci.

We discuss the rain, of course. The weather and the triumphant Garçon are the subjects of the day. Then Clarke says that he and his "guys" are going to check out the kitchen once more.

"We can hang here," K. Burke volunteers.

And we do. We even have a serious discussion concerning the merits of crab cakes versus hush puppies. Then K. Burke, who must have been reading *Horse Racing for Dummies*, lectures me on the wonders of American Pharoah, the most recent horse to win the Triple Crown.

K. Burke ends her lecture abruptly and says, "I'm worried, Moncrief."

I shrug and say, "We have done all we can. They have put ten plainclothesmen at the stables after the training horse was killed. They put thirty officers in the crowd today, two of them directly behind the Savatiers and us. They randomly tested all the food. They did backgrounds on the caterers, waiters, band…"

"Moncrief!" K. Burke says. "Over there."

She points to two young men walking toward us, wearing jeans and yellow rain slickers, carrying either side of a huge arrangement of roses. Holy shit! The floral display is identical to the arrangement Marguerite Savatier received at the Kentucky Derby.

"Where'd these roses come from?" asks K. Burke.

"I don't know. Some kid, a teenager, dropped 'em off. Matt and I were just working out there, parking cars, trying to stay dry. Then this kid shows up in this shitty old van. He gives us each twenty bucks and tells us to bring it inside to the party. He says they're for some old lady."

He then pulls a small gift card from his pocket and hands the envelope to Burke who then passes it to me.

The roses are, of course, for Marguerite.

"You know where the old lady is?" says the guy who's helped carry in the floral arrangement.

"Yeah, we do," I say. "We'll make sure she gets them."

CHAPTER 24

BACK IN NEW YORK, at the Midtown East precinct, K. Burke and I receive an exceptionally warm welcome from our boss, Inspector Nick Elliott.

"Where the hell on Christ's green earth have you two lovebirds been?"

K. Burke now makes a huge mistake. She talks.

"Excuse me, Inspector Elliott. I just want to make it clear that Luc Moncrief and I are not—in any way, shape, or form—involved in a romantic or…"

Elliott interrupts.

"Thank you, Detective Burke. Your private life is your business."

K. Burke won't let go of it. Bad idea. She tries once more.

"This is the truth. Moncrief and I have never…"

Now Elliott interrupts loudly. No one is going to interrupt him again. He's moved back to the work discussion.

"As I was saying. Take a look at this. It's a surveillance video of a drug dealer in Central Park."

This time I speak.

"Inspector, forgive my rudeness, but finding a drug dealer in Central Park is as common as finding a blade of grass in Central Park."

"I don't disagree, Moncrief, but just take a look." Then he adds, "And do it quietly." By now both K. Burke and I have annoyed him.

Elliott motions to us with his finger from his desk chair. Burke and I move behind him and lean into the computer screen.

The black-and-white picture portrays—in muddy shades of light and dark gray—what looks like clouds. Eventually, as the scene comes into focus, everything is more easily identifiable as an unkempt area of trees and weeds and stone boulders.

"It looks like Sherwood Forest," Burke says. "Is it the Ramble?"

The Ramble is a wooded area of Central Park totally un-manicured and un-landscaped.

"Yup. During the day you see bird-watchers with their binoculars and notepads," says Elliott. Then, "At night it turns into a kind of playground for gay guys."

"I have been to this area. To the Ramble," I say.

Elliott looks up at me, slightly startled. Burke turns her head and looks at me. Also slightly startled.

"No. I am not a bird-watcher. But when I began working for you, Inspector, you may recall, my first assignment was searching for criminals who stole bicycles. For three weeks myself and Maria Martinez spent two days at the Bethesda Fountain, two days in the Sheep Meadow, and two days in the Ramble, all in pursuit of bicycle thieves."

"And as I remember, you and your partner didn't catch one goddamn bike thief," says Elliott.

"Ah, but I learned a great deal about the geography. Right now, in this video I can tell you the scene is located precisely between Harkness House on the East Side and the Museum of Natural History on the West Side."

"Great. Keep watching," says Elliott.

The camera suddenly makes a sharp downward turn. We zoom in for a medium close-up to record who is standing on the stone pathway that rambles through the Ramble.

Burke and I study the screen. It now shows a fairly sharp image—for a police surveillance video: a teenage boy. Tall, thin, with a great deal of blond hair. Perhaps he is seventeen.

"New York City rich kid," K. Burke says. "A common species."

She is correct. He wears a blue blazer with an indecipherable gold insignia on the front pocket. A white button-down shirt of the Brooks Brothers variety. Striped blue-and-yellow silk tie in a thin sloppy knot. Gray pants.

"In fact," she continues thoughtfully, "didn't we see one of those recently?"

I am distracted. "His rucksack is bursting," I say.

"Speak English, Moncrief," says Elliott. "What the hell is a *rucksack?*"

Burke cuts in again. "At Miss Tweddle's. Didn't we see…"

She trails off as two similarly dressed teenage boys approach. The blond boy reaches into his…backpack…and hands each of them a plastic bag.

"No exchange of money," says Burke. "Maybe the next customer."

"I think his clientele pay in advance or put it on the tab," says Elliott.

"The latter—the tab—that is the way the rich do it," I say.

No sooner has Burke predicted a 'next customer' than a pretty—and very curvy—brunette woman, maybe thirty years old, in athletic clothes approaches. Again, the blond boy reaches into his satchel and hands over a small plastic bag. And again no money is seen.

"This is why I called you to look at this," says Elliott. "Do you recognize that woman?"

"Oh, my God," says Burke. "The Monahans' nanny."

"Mrs. Meade-Grafton!" I remember her unsettling laughter.

"One of the officers who was at the Monahan apartment happened to be on this as well. Lucky stroke for us. Especially while you two are gallivanting around," Elliott says, with insinuation.

Burke's face is very red, but she lets it pass. "What I was going to say is that we saw two boys wearing blazers and gray pants exiting the elevator when we entered Miss Tweddle's building."

"Very good, Burke!" I exclaim. "I had forgotten. Your sartorial eye is getting better every day."

I do not think I deserve her glare.

We watch more transactions. Most of the buyers are young. Most of them are white. The entire video will continue for twelve minutes before the blond boy leaves the frame.

"We had no trouble identifying the teen pusher. He's been

booked before, petty thievery once. Ready for this? He and his girlfriend bolted a bill at Daniel. The most expensive restaurant in the city. Plainclothes caught them two blocks away on Fifth Avenue."

"Beware the couple who attend the restroom at the same time," I say.

Elliott smiles slightly and recites the rest of the rap sheet: Weed outside a dance club on 28th Street. Assault of another student at a school basketball game.

"And no arrests that stuck?" Burke says.

"No. The kid's name is Reed Minton Reynolds. His father, Bill Reynolds, is that big deal weight-loss specialist, and, if you want, he'll give you a side order of plastic surgery. I've met him twice—actually a nice guy. Full disclosure, he's also responsible for 50 percent of the funding for the Police Athletic League."

"And 50 percent of the facelifts and breast augmentations in Manhattan," K. Burke says.

I can't resist. I turn and say, "You sound like you know something about these procedures, K. Burke."

Elliott shoots me an angry look.

"Don't start." A pause. Enough time for K. Burke to give a *somebody got in trouble* kind of smile. Elliott continues.

"Anyway, this Reed Reynolds kid is about to graduate Dalton, and he's signed, sealed, and soon-to-be-delivered to Yale. I'd like you two to track him for a day or two or three. Stay close to him. I want you to see where he goes, if he works anywhere else in the park. Do a 'smother job' on him. I'm not that interested in him, but…I think if we get a good fix on him, we can find out who's supplying him with his stash."

K. Burke gives one of her energetic responses: "Gotcha, Inspector."

As we reach Elliott's office door to leave I cannot resist saying: "Oh, and by the way, Inspector. While we're in Central Park, I'll keep my eyes open for any stolen bicycles."

"Get the hell out of here, Moncrief."

"Gotcha, Inspector."

The last word I hear from Elliott's mouth is simple.

"Asshole!"

CHAPTER 25

Monday
3:15 p.m.

WE SPENT ALL YESTERDAY afternoon trying to track down this kid, but only saw him as he arrived at home at the end of the day, and never came back out. But we never saw him leave this morning, either, unless he left before dawn, so now K. Burke and I are waiting on the north side of East 89th Street. We watch students straggling out of the Dalton School. Some light cigarettes. Others hold hands. Reed Reynolds doesn't show.

"Let's get over to Central Park. Maybe he cut out of school early," I say.

"Or maybe he never went to school today," says Burke. "I remember my own last few days of high school. Once we got accepted to college or had a job lined up, we didn't care anymore."

We enter the park just south of the Metropolitan Museum. We walk over a wide grassy area where shirtless men and near-shirtless women are sunning themselves. We then make our way down a small dirt pathway that leads us into a large dark wooded area. The Ramble.

The skunky-sweet smell of weed is in the air. Burke and I quickly locate the general area where Reed Reynolds was recorded distributing drugs. A few people are around—tourists, dog-walkers—but there are others in more secluded corners, kissing and smoking. But it's the same as the wait at his house this morning and at his school this afternoon—no Reed Reynolds.

I suggest we walk farther into the woods. It pays off. Thank you, instinct. A slightly swampy overgrown area, a few people, a few pairs of people. And there he is, holding court on a bench, like a little kid running a lemonade stand. We watch, taking care to remain hidden in the trees.

There he is, smoking cigarettes, an occasional finger snap to the beat of the music coming through his phone. He pauses only when a buyer comes along. Reynolds hands out his little zip-lock bags, his plastic orange bottles of bennies or red balls or good-old reliable speedballs. He's got a steady flow of customers. He seems to know exactly what they came for. No money changes hands. In about twenty minutes he's supplied about a dozen people.

Who are these folks? Your basic mixed bag of New Yorkers: the old, the young, the black, the white. Some are dressed for sleeping on the street. Some are dressed for sleeping at the Carlyle. They're as varied as the crowd at a Knicks game. People like Mara Monahan and Tessa Fulbright, two of those young women who died, would fit seamlessly into this group.

"You're starting to get agitated, Moncrief," says K. Burke.

"It is true, K. Burke. I have a great agitation to put handcuffs on this little preppy shithead," I say.

"Our job right now is to watch him and follow him. Nothing more. Nothing less."

"Oui, maman," I say.

Suddenly, K. Burke elbows me.

"Take a look at that guy with Reynolds now," she says.

I look to see a middle-aged man in annoyingly good shape. Sinewy muscles and forearms. He is wearing a ridiculous costume: tight black lycra shorts, a colorful yellow bicycling shirt and a yellow helmet.

"I think that man has escaped from the circus," I say.

"No. He's that guy who gives massages. Remember that gift certificate you gave me for massages? That's him."

"Ah, *oui*. The Armenian masseur. Louis."

"*Non*. The Hungarian masseur. Laszlo."

"Whatever his name," I say, "he's spending my money on skag."

We study the other customers. Two of them are teenagers—very distressing. Two of the female purchasers are what are known as "yummy mummies," in a way that is also distressing.

We watch the ebb and flow of buyers.

"Aha, K. Burke," I suddenly say. "Now it is my turn to push my elbow into your side. You will please look at that woman who is approaching young Master Reynolds."

I point to an attractive Manhattan-type: Her perfectly cut chestnut-colored hair falls over a snug white T-shirt. She wears a pair of baggy black linen shorts. The woman is not beautiful, but she is impeccably put together. This woman is evidence of an observation my late beloved Dalia sometimes made: "She's done the best she can with what God gave her."

"Okay, Moncrief. Who is she?" asks K. Burke.

"You do not know her? You met her just a few days ago. She…"

"Holy shit!" says Burke, perhaps a little too loudly. "It's that frumpy English nanny…what's-her-name… the one who worked for what's-her-name."

"Well put, K. Burke. What's-her-name is correctly named Julia Highridge, who appears to have been transformed from a dowdy Miss Marple into a chic Manhattan mademoiselle."

"It's amazing how much better she looks," says Burke.

"A touch of makeup. And a six-hundred-dollar Frederic Fekkai haircut," I say.

Reed Reynolds hands Julia Highridge a plastic bag, and she walks in the direction of Central Park West. She seems to be the day's final customer.

Reed Reynolds stands alone. He makes a few quick notes on a small pad. Then he takes a silver flask from his bag and takes a long swig. He recaps the flask and slips it into his backpack. Reed Reynolds heads east to Fifth Avenue. He half walks. He half runs. He has youth on his side. We take off after him. Skipping, hopping, jogging, racing, or leaping over a stone wall, K. Burke and I keep up with him.

Now we're out of the park. He crosses Fifth Avenue. We stay on the Park side and watch him. Reynolds stops at 930 Fifth Avenue, a large gray-stone building. He nods to the doorman. The doorman touches the rim of his cap. Then Reed Reynolds enters the building.

He's home.

"Damn."

Now it is *my* turn to calm *her* down.

"K. Burke. Please. You will settle your nerves. We will follow him. Tomorrow. And the next day. We will learn from him. Then once we know how he does it and where he gets his inventory... *Voilà!*

"This young man believes he's going to Yale. But first... well, he may have to do an internship on Rikers Island."

CHAPTER 26

Tuesday
3:00 p.m.

EARLY THE NEXT MORNING, K. Burke and I visit the office of Megan Scott, the Dean of Students at the Dalton School. We have shown her our ID and begin our questions, politely of course.

"We need to know if Reed Reynolds was in class today," we say.

"Why do you *need* to know?" asks Megan Scott.

"That's an expression, Miss Scott," says K. Burke. "And this is an NYPD investigation."

Burke and I know that many of the students at this school are the children of the rich and powerful. That means little to me, and it means absolutely nothing to my partner.

"We give information out on our students only when it's necessary," says Megan Scott.

"Mademoiselle," I say. "We have asked you for one piece of information. Was the boy in school today? That is not an inflammatory or provocative question."

Burke gives me a look that seems to say, "We're not going to let this bureaucrat obstruct our investigation."

"Very well," says Scott. "Reed was *in* class today, but he was not in this building. He's finishing up a special project at the

Metropolitan Museum of Art. Okay. There's your answer. Now if I may ask a question, what's the problem?"

"Not a problem, really. We just want to talk to him," Burke says.

"This Reed Reynolds, he is a good student, a good young man?" I ask, trying hard to use as much French charm as I can muster.

"Yes, 'this Reed Reynolds' is a very good student. He's on his way to Yale. He's a wonderful young man. If you could see this project he's doing with the curator of Dutch Renaissance portraiture at the Met…"

K. Burke has heard all she cares to hear. She puts an end to it.

"Thanks, Miss Scott. Thanks for letting us take up your precious time," she says.

Later that day, we're back in the Ramble, witnessing a similar-looking stream of buyers.

Reed Reynolds is still, of course, totally prepped out—white button-down, striped tie, loafers. He looks like he should be on the front of a prep school recruitment brochure.

We watch the distribution of the plastic bags of…heroin? Weed? Speed? Buttons? The possibilities are endless.

Then I turn to Burke and say, "Okay. I'm going to try something."

"What?" she asks.

"I think I'll make a purchase," I say.

"It won't work, Moncrief. These are regulars. Don't be stupid."

I know that she's right, but there's nothing to lose. And if I make a buy we can hook him into cuffs without chasing all over the city. As I walk toward him, I can practically *hear* K. Burke rolling her eyes.

"I was wondering if you could help me out?" I say.

"Probably not," he says. His voice is flat, dead, weak.

"Maybe just some loose weed," I say.

"No."

"I have two hundred dollars."

"No, man. Go away."

"Five hundred for two ounces?"

This time he doesn't even bother to say "no." He simply walks away.

I return to K. Burke.

"Please notice, Moncrief. I am not saying a word."

But Reed Reynolds doesn't go far, once he sees I'm gone. We watch from our hiding place as, like yesterday, he makes some brief notes and then takes a swig from his silver flask. This time, he does not head toward the Upper East Side but heads south through the park. We tail him past the lake, past Bethesda Fountain, on through the Sheep Meadow, then we are out of the park.

At 59th Street, just opposite the Plaza Hotel, Reed Reynolds hails a cab. We do the same. We follow them down Seventh Avenue, to the downtown corner where it changes to Varick Street. We're in SoHo now.

Reed Reynolds gets out of his cab at 300 Spring Street, a cement and steel monstrosity, a modernistic pile of crap in the midst of the great old SoHo iron-clad buildings.

Burke is on her iPad.

Seconds later she says, "It's his father's office and clinic. William Reynolds, MD. Let's go up. We can take a service elevator, maybe, or…"

"No," I say. "I know something better to do. And *you* will do it tomorrow."

"Me?" she asks. Burke looks confused. And suspicious.

"You will visit the eminent plastic surgeon, Dr. William Reynolds, *and* you will see if he will sell you some drugs."

"I'm not so…"

"Come, come, K. Burke. I can tell… You also think it is a good idea."

"Well…maybe…yes," she says. (Oh, how she hates to agree with me.)

"And for now I have another good idea."

"And that is?" she asks, also suspiciously.

"We are a mere three blocks from Dominique Ansel Bakery. Let's go and have some good coffee *and* one of Ansel's famous cronuts. *Allons-y!* Let's go!"

"I know how to speak French!" she explodes.

"Please, no angry attitude, K. Burke. Let's hurry! The bakery may soon be out of cronuts."

CHAPTER 27

I HAVE JUST SHARED with K. Burke my precise plan for tomorrow morning. The blueprint is not without some danger. And Burke will be the major player, practically the only player.

"Have you cleared any of this with Inspector Elliott?" K. Burke asks. I think she is nervous. And I don't blame her.

"Share it with Elliott? Of course not," I say. "I have cleared it with you, and I have already cleared it with myself. I think that will be sufficient approval."

"Sweet Jesus, Moncrief," she says.

We walk a few steps to the children's playground next door to Dominique Ansel Bakery. We begin eating our extraordinary cronuts.

As I watch the children in the wading pool and beneath the gentle sprinkler, I am transported—but just for a few moments—to that small unknown children's area in the Jardin du Luxembourg, a mostly hidden area of slides and swings and climbing ropes, an area where a grumpy old man performs absolutely terrible puppet shows, a childhood memory that…

"Moncrief, the plan. You were about to give me the details," Burke says.

My memory of the Jardin du Luxembourg explodes into the New York air, and I tell Burke the plan.

She will make an appointment to visit Dr. William Reynolds, father of drug dealer Reed Reynolds. Only an hour earlier we followed the son to his father's medical office. Only yesterday we watched an employee of one of the beautiful dead women purchase drugs from Reed Reynolds. Beyond that, we know that Dr. Reynolds is the go-to weight-loss specialist for the wealthy women of Manhattan.

"Listen, K. Burke. You are perfect for this job. You are attractive. You are slender. You are articulate. You are the perfect 'insecure rich woman.' We will buy you some decent clothing..."

Burke sneers a very tiny sneer. "Watch it, Moncrief."

"What did I say?"

"Just go on."

"No. It is simple. You go in. You say you are interested in...oh, I don't know...a little Botox here...a little lifting of the butt... maybe you discuss the nose, although I must say that your nose is a sweet little button, a gift from your Irish ancestors."

"Okay, Moncrief, let's stop right there," she says. "I'm actually with you on this idea. I hate to admit it, but it's good. As an idea. But I'm going to change something. Instead of surgery, I'll try asking Dr. Reynolds for drugs—weight-loss, relaxants, stimulants, that sort of thing."

"It is your setup and your scene. It is all up to you," I say.

I have been googling around on diet and weight-loss sites. I have learned about, I tell Burke, a desire on some women's parts to supplement their amphetamines and appetite suppressants with laxatives. I hand Burke my iPad. She reads a highlighted piece from Dr. William Reynolds's website, BeautifulYouInstantly.com.

Some patients believe that the additional use of diuretics and laxatives aids in reaching their weight-loss goal. This is a matter in which I try to dissuade them. Strong emetic medication, while fostering the sense of weight-loss, is a worthless medical methodology.

"But you're contradicting yourself. Reynolds is saying here that he does *not* approve of laxatives…" says Burke.

"*C'est vrai*. That is true, but my instinct tells me this: I am beginning to suspect that our four victims were using very strong purgatives. Such medications either contributed to their death or actually caused their death. Reynolds is invoking the 'reverse psychology' approach. Tell someone they don't need something, and, of course…"

Burke finishes my sentence: "And, of course, they will want it even more."

"Here's what I think. You remember the ME's reports, yes? No drugs, they said…except for an antidepressant or two, and a seemingly innocent laxative. So what do I think? That our victims died of laxative overdosing."

"Oh, my God," says Burke.

I continue. "I also believe, consciously or not, that he was supplying his son's business with items that have street value. But to our victims, he supplied massive doses of laxatives—over-the-counter, prescription, even holistic herbs and teas. In any event when you go to see Reynolds, ask him to sell you one or two of the high-powered laxatives. Okay?"

I can see that Burke's enthusiasm is growing stronger.

"I'll do it, Moncrief, but I'm nervous."

"Not to have the worry. I will be there. I'll have a SWAT team on standby. Emergency medical will be standing by," I say.

"Medical?"

"Precautions, K. Burke. Laxatives can be…unpredictable." She doesn't laugh at my joke. "Don't worry. It is a harmless setup."

"Well if it's so easy, why don't you do it, Moncrief?"

I cannot resist. I say, "I would not be credible. What possible imperfection could Dr. Reynolds find in me?"

"Maybe he could change you from a smug asshole into a normal person," she says. Neither of us speaks for a moment.

"I will call." I dial the number from the website. A receptionist with a warm, calm voice answers. I exaggerate my French accent.

"Yes, I'd like to make an appointment for my client. She has not seen Dr. Reynolds before, but he is highly recommended. I am afraid my client needs to be seen right away—as in tomorrow. Her name is Marion Cotillard. Can you fit her in?"

I watch Burke's eyes widen. "Oh, you can? Thank you. She will see you tomorrow at 5:00."

I hang up and she sputters, "Marion Cotillard?! She's a famous actress! I don't look anything like her."

"Does not matter," I say. "Now you're in. We never said you were *that* Marion Cotillard."

"What about when they ask for my identification?"

"You will have this."

I hand her a rolled-up wad of cash.

"Take this. Buy everything with cash."

"Why? The NYPD never allows personal money to…" she begins.

I ignore her. "It is thirty one-hundred-dollar bills. Three thousand dollars. Take it, and use it."

K. Burke nods. She takes the cash. We finish our cronuts and coffee.

Now the only thing left to do is to persuade K. Burke to walk with me to Alexander Wang and buy an outfit that's just a little bit more chic than her khaki pants and Old Navy yellow polo shirt.

"The weather is cooler," I say. "Let's walk around SoHo for a little bit."

"Sure," she says. "And while we're walking, let's stop at Alexander Wang and buy me some very cool clothes."

I laugh. Then I say, "You are something else, Katherine. I know that this plan will go very well."

"Holy shit," she says. "You must think this is important."

"And you say that because?"

"Because you actually called me Katherine."

CHAPTER 28

BURKE BLUSHED BUT WAS secretly proud when Nick Elliott first intro-
duced her to Moncrief: "She learned it, she earned it. She's one
of the best detectives around. *And* she's got guts to go with her
brains." She knew it was true. She didn't often have the chance to
do undercover operations, and was looking forward to this. Even
so, Burke couldn't help feeling nervous about this operation.

She walks into Dr. William Reynolds's office the next day at
4 p.m., and her mind's eye virtually clicks a photograph of the
waiting room—furnished with objects she only recognizes due to
Moncrief's shopping addiction.

Creamy white walls. Two authentic—Le Corbusier, she
thinks?—black leather couches facing each other. A glass-topped
coffee table sitting between the couches. An authentic and huge
photograph hanging on the wall that Burke recognizes thanks to
an art crime case. It's Jeff Koons's *Made in Heaven*—a near-naked
man and woman in a passionate embrace.

The couches, the Koons. Click. Brain picture.

Burke is the only patient in the waiting room. A receptionist
sits behind a glass Parsons table. The only item on her table is a
very small MacBook Air. Next to the table is a small gray cabinet.

The receptionist is gorgeous. Long blond hair. Perfect features on a perfectly shaped face. Burke remembers what her mother used to say about a beautiful woman or a handsome man: "God took extra care when He put that one together." The receptionist wears a simple sleeveless gray shift, matching the gray cabinet. Nice touch.

Burke approaches, and as she gets closer she notices a slightly theatrical shininess to the woman's face. Could she really be using pancake makeup? Greasepaint? The woman's figure is not merely thin, it is thinner than thin. Her clavicles are sharp and prominent.

The receptionist is possibly twenty-five years old, or thirty-five, or forty-five…Burke really cannot tell. The receptionist exists in plastic surgery time.

"Ms. Cotillard, welcome," she says. A warm voice, a quiet voice. Burke senses disappointment, but there is no comment. A moment later she is filling out forms on a tablet—the information is fictional, but she trusts she would be done before this was discovered. After a short wait, the receptionist leads Burke into a changing room. Burke slips into an unusually elegant examination gown—pale yellow, soft thick cotton, matching slippers.

A knock on the changing room door.

A man's voice. "Miss Cotillard. It's Bill Reynolds. May I come in?"

Burke opens the door. William Reynolds is a bigger-sized cosmetically enhanced version of his son the drug dealer. No classic white doctor coat and stethoscope here. His blond hair is perfectly cut, his black suit fits perfectly, and his shirt is bespoke, like Moncrief's, allowing his slim frame to show some muscle.

He shakes Burke's hand. Reynolds does not indulge in ordinary clichés of greeting, no "Nice to meet you," no "Good to see you."

Instead he tenderly moves both his hands to Burke's shoulders and speaks gently: "Let me help you, Marion. Will you please let me help you?"

It should sound creepy, she thinks, but instead it sounds soothing. Burke wants to hear something dangerous or, at the very least, phony. Instead his voice makes her feel restful, trusting, and…oh, shit, she thinks…ever so slightly aroused.

CHAPTER 29

"MY OFFICE IS THIS way. Please, come with me, so we can talk before the exam."

Why am I wearing a gown? Through another door. Reynolds's office is sparse: another glass desk, a small gray cabinet. Some solemn-looking medical books on the shelves. An examining table with three measuring tapes and a small camera. Nothing else. It barely reads like a doctor's office. Reynolds gestures to the chair opposite his desk.

"What is your trouble? What is your dream? How can I help?" he asks.

She knows she must slip into the role she has come here to play. Reynolds's voice soothes her. But, damn it, she will, of course, be tougher. She's smarter. Clear the decks. Light the lights.

"I am just starting to hate the way I look. I mean, I know I'm sort of pretty. I also know the world's falling apart, and I'm worrying about the millimeter droop in my neck and my ears. But, well, I guess I should start by doing something about my weight…"

Burke knows that she is perfectly proportioned. She knows that if she ever truly complained to her cousins Maddy and Marilyn they'd laugh and criticize her for such self-involvement. God forbid she ever said something to Moncrief. He would force-feed her a hot fudge sundae.

"There's always room for improvement," Reynolds says. "That's the wonder of life."

That's the wonder of life? Burke thinks. *Jesus.*

Reynolds reaches into his filing cabinet and takes out two pamphlets. He hands one to her.

"Read along with me, Marion. Let's start on page three."

The page is titled "Help on Your Journey."

He begins reading:

"The judicious use of diet pills may lend you exactly the support you and your willpower need in order to learn and maintain sensible eating habits. Small doses of Dexedrine in limited quantities will give you the resilience you never knew you had."

Burke nods. Dexedrine, huh? On the street, in the clubs, in the best and worst neighborhoods, they're called Black Beauties.

"By the way," he says. "I know, of course, that my assistant, Nora, asked for the name of your pharmacy. That will be used strictly for emergencies. I will, for the sake of precision, put together a weekly packet of medication for you. It's a much wiser system, a safer system."

"But how do you know what…" Burke begins.

"I know, Marion. The Reynolds system is always the same, always foolproof. When you see a truly beautiful woman on Fifth Avenue, chances are great that she once sat where you're sitting now." He continues reading, in what is becoming the most bizarre doctor's visit she's ever had:

> *"Random and unpredictable sleeplessness is sometimes the result of even the most well-planned and supervised weight-loss plans, like the one you'll be embarking on. To compensate for the possible problem of insomnia, you will also be prescribed limited doses of Flunitrazepam, the medication that has been proven helpful to many European women."*

Again Burke nods. She is sure that she remembers Moncrief saying that Flunitrazepam is called *le petit ami parfait,* "the perfect boyfriend," by wealthy Parisian women.

The reading from the gospel according to Reynolds continues. He tells Burke that her pill packet will also contain two forms of mescaline, as well as what Reynolds calls "a late afternoon relaxant."

Burke knows that on the streets of New York, these tablets are called roofies.

Reynolds stands at his desk.

"So that's it," he says. "I'll see you a week from today, anytime that's convenient and available."

"That's it?" she says, and she realizes that she may have sounded too surprised. Quickly she adds, "What I mean is: aren't you going to weigh me or take blood or urine or look in my eyes?"

"No need to right now. If we need those things at a later date, then we'll do them. But for now, it's better to just relax."

He hands her a small bag. It is made of a gray velvet-like material. The bag has a gold thread closure; it looks like it would contain a piece of silver given as a wedding gift, or a piece of jewelry given to a loved one.

Then Reynolds hands her a five-by-seven manila envelope. The envelope has nothing but the letter *A* written on it.

"These are helpful also. They're a mild laxative. Sometimes my clients find the act of bowel emission to be a helpful signal of how they're doing."

Burke has studied Moncrief's notes. She knows exactly what this medication is: Amatiza, a prescription laxative.

Reynolds keeps talking. "They're fairly large pills. So be sure to take plenty of water with them. Of course, you'll be staying away from all fruit juice. Too much sugar. Sugar and carbs. The dual enemy."

As he speaks she cannot resist squeezing the metal tab on the manila envelope. She pulls out one of the light-blue pills. By any estimation it is huge.

"Can I cut these in half?" Burke asks.

"You may get them down any way you choose," he says. "Put them on the tip of your husband's…" he begins to say. Then he laughs. Burke tries hard not to show that she's both surprised and repulsed by his joke.

"In any event, the medication chart for when you should take these pills is in the little bag," he says. "If you have any questions, Nora or I are always available."

Reynolds removes his suit jacket. He hangs it carefully on the back of his desk chair. He walks around the desk to where Burke is seated.

She thinks: *Why am I wearing an examination gown if he's not going to examine me?*

Now Dr. Reynolds stands in front of her, close to her.

"Do you have any questions?" he asks.

"No, I guess not," Burke asks.

But she realizes that this is now or never. She's got to get him to *sell* her some drugs. She pretends as if some new thought has just crossed her mind.

"Oh, yes. There is something. I'm glad you brought up the laxative thing," she says.

"Yes?"

"A friend of mine told me she occasionally uses something called…oh, I'm not sure…it's like…clementine…clemerol… some sort of laxative that really relaxes you inside…she says."

Burke is setting herself up to request an illegal drug, one banned by the FDA. It should be powerful. It's formulated for horses.

"You're probably thinking of Clenbuterol," Reynolds says. "And it *is* highly effective. But I'm not sure it 'relaxes you inside.'"

"I could swear that's what she said."

"It could help. Some women like it."

"I'd give it a try. I'm pretty serious about losing weight."

"I'll add it to the prescription package. But I must warn you…"

Oh, Burke thinks, this is when he warns me of serious side effects.

No. Reynolds says, "…that there will be an extra charge. I'll give you seven pills, until next week's visit. Like I say, they're pricey. One hundred dollars each."

"That's fine," says Burke.

"Very well. Now go get dressed, and on your way out stop and see Nora. I'll tell her to add Clenbuterol to your 'goody bag.' It's been a pleasure meeting you."

"Same here," Burke says.

With a big smile on his face, Dr. William Reynolds speaks again. "Next week we can discuss what we might do about those droopy breasts of yours."

CHAPTER 30

KATHERINE BURKE DRESSES QUICKLY. The baggy black linen Alexander Wang pants tie easily at the waist. The simple white cotton T-shirt slips quickly over her shoulders. She grabs her pocketbook and she does a fast check of its contents: iPad, personal iPhone, work cell phone, roll of thirty hundred-dollar bills, and finally, the "Austrian Baby," which is what Moncrief calls the Glock 19 handgun that Burke and Moncrief carry.

Burke walks down the short hallway to the waiting room. She is certain that the lighting is dimmer than when she first entered. Yes, her quick police detective mind registers that the two Sonneman table lamps have been turned off. The track lighting has been turned down. The spotlight on the Koons photo is no longer on.

"It's not scary," she thinks. "It's just gloomy."

The very skinny, very pretty receptionist/assistant—Reynolds called her Nora—is not at the glass desk.

Then suddenly a noise, a human sound, not quite a cough, not quite a sniffle. Burke turns in the direction of one of the black couches. The back of the couch is facing her. Then Burke watches the receptionist beginning to sit up. Nora yawns the tiniest of yawns.

"Oh, Miss Cotillard, I'm sorry. I was just catching a nap while I was waiting for you. You're Dr. Reynolds's last patient. Forgive me," she says as she stands.

"What's to forgive? I wish I could grab a nap right now myself," says Burke.

Nora goes to her desk and begins tapping away at her iPad. "Let's just see what the total payment is. The consultation is one thousand…"

One thousand!

Burke tries not to show her astonishment when she hears the amount.

"The weight-loss medical package is another thousand," says Nora. "And I see here that Dr. Reynolds has dispensed additional medication, Clenbuterol. That's seven…"

Now Burke hears a noise coming from behind her. Nora must be hearing that noise also. Both women look toward the black couch where Nora had been napping. The cough comes again, louder. It is an intense cough, a man's cough, a sick man's cough, Burke thinks.

Suddenly a young man stands up. Burke can only assume that he also has been lying on that couch. The young man squints in the direction of both women. He seems confused, disoriented. He is blond, young, thin. The young man is Reed Reynolds.

"That's Dr. Reynolds's son. I think they're meeting for dinner," says Nora, who delivers the information calmly, matter-of-factly. Burke nods, as if this actually explained something.

"Your dad will be out momentarily, Reed," says Nora. Now she looks back to her iPad and says, "That will be a total of twenty-seven hundred dollars, Miss Cotillard."

Katherine Burke begins counting out hundred-dollar bills.

"Excellent," says Nora. "Cash."

Burke speaks. "Oh, and I'll need a receipt."

"I'll just e-mail it to you," says Nora.

"Oh, I'd prefer a hard copy."

"If I e-mail it you can just print it at home."

"Yes, but I really would prefer to leave with a piece of paper. I'm a dinosaur when it comes to receipts."

Suddenly a loud harsh voice comes from Reed Reynolds.

"Are you deaf *and* stupid, lady? She said she's going to e-mail it to you."

"Reed, please…" says the receptionist.

The young man comes from around the black couch and approaches the glass desk.

"I know this bitch," says Reed Reynolds. "She doesn't *know* that I know her, but I do."

"I don't remember ever meeting you," says Burke, who is now really on edge. This kid is stoned or at least buzzed.

"You were with that asshole who tried to buy shit from me in the park. Like I didn't know you were feds or cops or some other kind of asshole."

Burke is not quite certain what she should say. But facing Reynolds, her arms and hands are shaking. Her stomach is churning. This operation is about to go up in flames. She turns away from Reed Reynolds to face Nora.

"Just ignore him," Nora says.

But Burke cannot. Reed Reynolds is walking toward her. His long legs bend dramatically at the knees. His walk is almost cartoonish.

The combination of sneer-and-smile on Reynolds's mouth, the dramatic deep red outline of his dead eyes…there's nothing cartoonish about that.

She snaps open her pocketbook. She reaches in, but immediately realizes that her cell phone is in the compartment where her Glock should be.

Reynolds's voice comes at her, loud but slurred: "Move to the goddamn door, lady."

Burke freezes.

Reynolds's voice again: "Get her! Are you fucking deaf? Get her."

It takes Burke a millisecond to realize that Reynolds is shouting at Nora.

If the cell phone is sitting where the Glock should be, then the Glock should be where the…

Burke reaches into her pocketbook. Yes. I am a lucky sonofabitch, she thinks. Burke spins to face Nora.

Nora is holding a gun.

Burke's arm is still in her bag. Her hand is on the gun. But Nora is a second ahead of her. Nora aims her pistol in Burke's general direction.

Nora fires—and misses. The bullet hits the couch.

This is astonishing…to everyone except a cop. *"The 'general direction' IS NEVER GOOD ENOUGH!"* She can hear her firearms instructor's voice.

"Even if you're only three feet from your target it's still READY, AIM, and SHOOT. If you forget the AIM part, then chances are you're dead."

Katherine Burke does what Nora didn't do.

First she *aims*. And then she shoots.

Blood sprays from Nora's neck. She falls on top of the desk. Nora's blood is smearing like children's finger paint on the glass desk.

Then suddenly a hideous, retching, gagging sound comes from Reed. Sick and savage and loud, like a cannibal war-cry.

Now Burke is alive in a kind of crazy way. She spins around and sees the boy fold at the waist. His head is almost at the floor, but he is still standing. He begins spewing a fountain of vomit, which splashes to the floor. Some of it hits his black pants as she uses her phone to call for Moncrief.

CHAPTER 31

I DIAL 911 AS I enter the reception room, along with Dr. William Reynolds. I see a dead woman face-down and bleeding out over a glass desk. I barely recognize Reed Reynolds, who is so unconscious that he appears to be dead, his head resting in his own pool of vomit. I ignore William Reynolds, staring at his dead receptionist and son. They will be dealt with when more officers arrive, which should be any minute.

When I look to the other corner, I see K. Burke standing, looking out the window. Her shoulders are shaking. She is sobbing, really sobbing, big bursts of tears mixed with squeaks and grunts and coughs.

I walk to her and from behind I put my arms on her shoulders and gently turn her around. She puts her head on my chest.

"It is all right, K. Burke. You behaved admirably. You have much to be proud of," I say softly.

I hold her, rubbing her back with my hands. Silence. Seconds. Minutes. Then Burke speaks.

"Moncrief, I just killed someone."

I imagine page after page after page of police forms and reports. Thousands of finger taps on so many cell phones and laptops.

Photographers and photographs and the whooshing sounds of expensive cameras. More detectives. Medical examiners. More police officers. Inspector Elliott. A deputy mayor. The newscasters. The newswriters. The news photographers. The people in the neighborhood. The conversations.

"They say they killed Dr. Reynolds."

"No. Not Reynolds. They killed his girlfriend."

"No. They killed the nurse."

"The nurse *is* the girlfriend."

I can see in my head what is coming, a spectacle for a summer's night in New York City.

I tell Burke that I will take her home to her apartment, and, to my mild surprise, she does not object. She does, however, remain completely silent as the patrol car takes us from SoHo to her apartment in the East 90s.

At her apartment door we step over the messy pile of shoes, boots, and magazines.

"What sort of alcoholic beverages do you have here?" I ask.

"There's a bottle of Dewar's in the cabinet over the fridge, and there's some Gallo Hearty Burgundy next to it," she says. She cannot see the disgust on my face when she mentions the wine. But this, of course, is hardly a time for humor, even between such great friends. Also, these are the first words she has spoken since we left the mad carnival in Dr. William Reynolds's office. Reynolds has been taken to the precinct. Burke has been brought to her home. All has ended the way it should. Yet the air is heavy with misery.

Burke pauses only a few feet into the apartment. She stands perfectly still. Her hands hang at her side.

"K. Burke, what can I do to help you?" I ask. "We have had no nourishment since luncheon. I will order something. A little soup, some bread, some pastry."

"Nothing," she says. Her voice is soft.

"Do you need to refresh yourself? Do you want me to draw you a bath?"

Burke turns her head toward me. She speaks, "'Draw me a bath.' You said 'Draw me a bath.' That's so old-fashioned. So foreign. So…Moncrief-like."

"Well, what is your answer? A bath? A shower? A Dewar's on the rocks?"

It looks as if a small smile is creeping onto her face. I am delighted. The breaking of the ice, as they say. But I'm very wrong. The smile continues without a stop. It curves up and over her cheeks. Her eyes squint hard. Her entire face becomes contorted into sadness. Tears. Loud. Shaking shoulders. Hands to face. Then through her tears comes her ragged voice.

"I think she would have shot me, Moncrief. Do you think so? Moncrief, tell me that you think if I had waited she would have killed me."

I grab her by the arms. And I speak sternly.

"You do *not* have to ask me or torture yourself. You did what your job called for you to do."

She leans onto my shoulder. She sobs, but the sobs do not last long.

"I want to take a shower," she says.

"That is wise," I say. "Perhaps it will help to wash the day away."

"Perhaps," she says. Then, "Thank you for helping. You don't have to stay. I'll be fine."

"No," I say. "I will wait until you are ready for sleeping. I will have a Dewar's waiting for you when you come out of your shower."

Before she enters her tiny bathroom K. Burke turns to me. Her smile is small, but it is real. She speaks. "Draw me a bath? I don't think anyone has ever said that to me." She closes the bathroom door.

The room I'm left in is cluttered with small piles of clothing, an opened but unmade Murphy bed, stacks of magazines, a desk computer whose screen frame is littered with decals and Post-it notes.

I am suddenly thinking: *Who is this woman and what has she become to me? A friend? Of course. A sister? Somewhat. A daughter? Absurd. A woman who might be my lover? No answer to that one. More "no" than "yes." But maybe not.*

I walk to the bathroom door. I hear the shower. Somehow the mere sound of the shower water raining down helps soothe me also.

I do not believe that time heals everything, but in this case, this time…I so very much hope and pray that it will. This is not just anybody in my life. This is Katherine.

CHAPTER 32

I STAY THE NIGHT.

K. Burke and I drink our glasses of scotch. She lies down on the "always-down" Murphy bed. I retreat to the green Barcalounger, which, I discover, is both incredibly ugly *and* incredibly comfortable.

When Detective Burke finishes her drink she holds out her glass. I move to the tiny kitchen area to pour more scotch. I'm gone maybe thirty seconds, but K. Burke is sound asleep when I get back.

I remove my shoes, my socks, my shirt.

I do not remember falling asleep. But I certainly do remember being awakened by the buzzing of my cell phone. I am not exactly surprised by the caller.

"Luc, as always we call at the most inconvenient time. It is me, Nicolas." I glance quickly at the Felix the Cat clock on Burke's wall and see that it is ten minutes after three in the morning.

"Wait just one moment," I whisper. I take the phone into the bathroom and close the door so not to wake K. Burke. I still keep my voice low.

"Yes, yes. What is the problem?" I ask.

"It is the same. Only different. We are here in New York City, as you know, of course, for the upcoming Belmont. We are at the St. Regis, and…all of this is *très mal*…this…" he begins. I want to scream "Get to the point." Then mercifully, the inevitable occurs: I hear Marguerite say, *"Donne-moi le téléphone, Nicolas."* And Nicolas gives Marguerite the telephone. She begins talking.

"Luc, do you know what the time of day is?" she says.

Oh, shit. Is she going to be polite and long-winded also?

But I stay cool. Instead of saying, "Of course I know what the goddamn time is," I say, "Yes. Tell me the problem."

"There was a phone call from the lobby desk. Just a few minutes ago. The man at the desk said that there was a delivery for us. He said that the deliveryman insisted it be brought up to the room immediately. We are, you know, traveling without a maid or a secretary. So Nicolas answered the door buzzer and…*Voilà!*" She pauses.

This time I do not edit or censor my reaction.

"What was it, goddamnit?"

"An extraordinary wreath of roses. Hundreds of them. Hundreds and hundreds. Just like the roses we previously received."

"A card? A message?"

"Yes. I shall read it to you," she says. "'Lose at Belmont. Or suffer the consequences.'"

I am silent. I am thinking. Then I say: "But of course. In the past they have delivered the roses at the victory party. This time they are certain that there will be no victory party."

Silence. Then Marguerite's voice again on the phone.

"Luc, are you still there?"

"Yes," I say. But I'm not completely *there*. My brain is traveling—filtering and sorting and clicking away. But it clicks slowly. I am weary from lack of sleep. My skin is wet with sweat. My eyes burn. My instincts fail to bring cohesion to my brain.

Marguerite's voice is just short of frantic. "What should we do, Luc?"

"Go back to bed. Try to sleep. I shall stop by your suite at 9 a.m."

"Is there nothing else for us to do until then?" she asks.

"Yes. There is one thing."

"Of course," says Marguerite.

"Order coffee and croissants for a nine o'clock room service, and tell them to make certain that the coffee is very strong and the croissants are very flaky."

CHAPTER 33

I DO NOT FALL back to sleep. K. Burke, however, sleeps soundly. Indeed, she is still sleeping when I leave her apartment at 7 a.m.

Back at my own place, a shower, a shave, fifteen minutes in the sauna, another shower, and then a phone call to Jimmy Kocot, the man who is known as "Bookie to the Stars." He is so named because he does not accept bets below a thousand dollars. Further, he does not necessarily accept your bet if he does not personally care for the person placing the bet. How do I know all this? Via the recommendation of Inspector Elliott.

Yes, I know. Amazing. My police boss recommended my bookie. Here's how: Approximately one year ago I told Nick Elliott that I had a good friend who was competing in a—don't think me too foppish—cribbage tournament in Lyon. Because there was a one-day electronics strike in France I could not get through online or by phone to place a "win" on my friend.

Inspector Elliott said that he sometimes used a bookie ("Betting isn't really betting unless you can bet odds," he said, by way of explanation of his own breaking of the law). And so I spoke with Jimmy Kocot. I bet five thousand euros on my friend Pierre Settel. And so I lost five thousand euros.

"So, you got another frog buddy in a cribbage match, Mr. Moncrief?" Jimmy asks this morning when I call.

"No. I'm interested in the Belmont Stakes," I say.

"So's everyone else," he says.

"A great deal of wagering?" I ask.

"A very great deal," he says.

"What sort of odds are you giving on Garçon?"

"I'm not. The smart money is on Millie's Baby Boy and Rufus. They're both three-to-one to win. My clients are not keen on Garçon. I couldn't tell you why."

"No idea?" I ask.

"No. I've got no clue. But the other two nags are coming in, like I say, three-to-one for winning."

"And nothing new to cause this change?" I ask.

There is a pause. When Jimmy speaks again his voice is quieter, intimate, almost a whisper.

"Two guys told me the horse has a sesamoid fracture. That's the bones down around…"

I finish his sentence, "…the ankles."

"Ridiculous," I say. "I'm going with Garçon. I know the owners, and they've told me nothing," I say.

"Whatever you want. I make my money either way. If you'd rather listen to those two old French people instead of me, it's your loss." He says it as a joke, but there is a note of malice in the joke.

"In any event, what are the odds on Garçon?"

"I've got him at seven-to-one."

"I'll take it," I say.

"You say you don't know any inside stuff, but I'm sure you know stuff that I don't know," says Jimmy Kocot, Bookie to the Stars. "Anyway, how much you betting?"

"Fifty thousand."

"You want to tell me that one more time?"

"I think you heard me."

"You doing a group bet, huh?"

"No. It's all mine."

"Fifty is a mighty big bet, even for me. How are you covering it? You know I can only do cash."

"You'll have it in less than a minute. I'll wire it to you right now."

Jimmy and I say our good-byes. I punch in the codes and numbers that deliver fifty thousand to a site called starsbook472ko.com.

CHAPTER 34

AN HOUR LATER, PERFECT luxury is on perfect display in the Savatiers' suite at the St. Regis on East 55th Street.

The elderly couple is, of course, dressed elegantly, Marguerite in a simple white suit with navy-blue piping, as if she had stepped out of a Chanel showroom in 1955. Nicolas in a dark-gray suit with a vest, a wide red silk tie with a diamond pin.

A waiter and waitress are pouring coffee into the exquisite St. Regis china cups—cups and plates that ironically are designed with a delicate border of roses.

Nicolas quickly reminds me that there are real and dangerous roses to deal with. "The floral arrangement is in the bedroom," says Nicolas.

I step into the adjoining bedroom—the beds are already made, the carpet already vacuumed. I check this arrangement of roses against the photographs from the Derby and the Preakness on my phone. Indeed, all three arrangements are identical.

When I return to the living room Marguerite thrusts the accompanying note toward me. A quick glance verifies that the request is to "Lose the Belmont." All I can do is read it and nod.

"Your croissants are getting cold, Luc," says Nicolas. There is a teasing smile on his face.

"My husband is not nearly so nervous as I am," says Marguerite, as we all sit down at the breakfast table.

"I am nervous, of course," explains Nicolas. "But what can happen to us? What are these 'consequences' we will suffer should we actually win—not lose—the Belmont tomorrow? Will they shoot us? So what? We will have won the Triple Crown. We have lived long and happy lives. People have died in far worse circumstances."

Marguerite sighs.

"No one loves her horses as much as I do, but I am not sure that I am willing to die for a horse race."

"Let me ask," I say. "Have you been in touch with the trainers and Belmont management about Garçon's health?"

"Of course, we speak to the head trainer every few hours. And our jockey Armand calls constantly…" begins Nicolas.

"He calls almost too often," Marguerite adds with a tiny laugh.

Nicolas: "And he is nervous but very optimistic about Saturday's race."

I am not surprised by this information. These trainers and Armand Joscoe have been with the Savatiers and their horses for many years. I nod, and then I take a big gulp of my coffee. I break off a crisp end piece from my croissant.

"Please, Luc. Tell us. What should we do?"

"First, we should finish our *petit déjeuner*. Then we should proceed as if all circumstances are normal. We will drive out to Long

Island and watch Garçon go through his paces. Then we can decide what to do."

"Just one more question," says Nicolas.

"And that is?"

"Where is the delightful Mademoiselle Burke?"

"Merci," I say. "How could I forget about her?" I click the contact list on my cell phone and call K. Burke.

"Where are you, Moncrief?" comes the very grumpy, very sleepy voice of K. Burke.

"I am at breakfast with the Savatiers, downtown. You must brush your teeth and comb your hair. Put on your clothing and put on a smiling, happy face. The Savatiers and I will come fetch you in less than fifteen minutes."

"No way that I can…"

"We are on our way out to Belmont," I say.

"I don't know, Moncrief. I don't think I can."

"Please, K. Burke. Life goes on. Today is a day for working."

CHAPTER 35

Belmont.
The day before the race.

THE MERCEDES SUV THAT carries Marguerite and Nicolas Savatier, K. Burke, and myself is allowed through three different gates. At the last gate hangs an enormous red-lettered sign:

WARNING: TRACK OFFICIALS, OWNERS, AND
EMPLOYEES ONLY BEYOND THIS POINT.

As we pass through, Marguerite says, "Now *that* is a sign to warm the heart of a frightened old lady."

I nod, but I am more taken with the exceptional beauty of Belmont racetrack—the hundreds of yards of lush ivy blanketing the walls, the freshly painted blue and white grandstand. Men and women in police uniform, men and women in official Belmont Park uniforms nod at us as we pass. The skies are cloudless and clear.

As we walk toward the stables I say, "The weather is a perfect seventy-seven degrees."

K. Burke catches sight of Nicolas's puzzled look and translates. "Seventy-seven degrees Fahrenheit is equal to about twenty-five degrees Celsius."

"Merci," says Nicolas. "I am afraid our beloved young friend

Luc has become transformed very much into the red-blooded American."

At the stable the Savatiers move as quickly as they are able toward Garçon. They stroke the horse's back. Nicolas looks into the horse's eyes.

There is a great deal of embracing and cheek-kissing between the Savatiers and the jockey, Armand Joscoe; between the Savatiers and *le docteur* Follderani, the vet that they've imported from France. Then begins the hugging and kissing between the owners and the trainers and the groomers. Finally, I receive a warm embrace from the jockey's tall son, Léon Joscoe. He looks very satisfied.

"Good to see you again, Léon," I say.

"And I'm tremendously happy to see you again, Monsieur Moncrief. It's been quite a ride for my father and me."

Now we have a great crowd of Frenchmen, all babbling excitedly at once. Actually a lovely occasion. Voices overlapping. Nervous laughter. Marguerite raises her voice; very unusual. Nicolas's eyes tear up; even more unusual.

K. Burke looks at me and says, "Okay. You win, Moncrief. I *do* speak French. But these folks are going way too fast for me. I don't understand very much."

"I assure you, it doesn't even make much sense to me."

Burke and I walk a few yards away from the small crowd of Frenchmen.

"So, we are alone for a moment. I am anxious to know: how are you feeling, K. Burke?" I ask.

"*Not* terrible," she says.

"*Not* terrible. Ah, compared to last night that is wonderful."

"And by the way," she says softly, "Thank you for helping me."

My voice now turns serious, a shift from banter between good friends.

"You shall feel even better in a very short while. I have deduced who it is that is threatening the Savatiers with the grotesque notes."

"You know who is…?" she begins. But I keep talking.

"*Ah, oui.* This must be the same person who murdered the training horse. The same person who has stolen all the joy and luster from winning the races. But that person is now done for."

"Who is it, Moncrief? How did you…"

"In a moment," I say. We move back near the French group.

I interrupt, but my voice has a genuine smile in it.

"Please, I must ask a favor of all of you: if you speak only French, please speak slowly. Better yet, if you can speak reasonable English, please try to do so. It would be helpful to all the Americans."

With a laugh Nicolas says, "Because English is the official language not only of our new American friend, Katherine Burke… but now it has also become the official language of our *old* American friend, Luc Moncrief."

Most of the crowd laughs.

Armand Joscoe, usually a quiet, shy man, says, "It is for me not much English. So I speak not much. But Léon speaks so good English. He will have to translate for me."

Almost everyone looks in the direction of Léon, who is fiercely tapping keys on his cell phone.

A sparse round of applause. Spirits are high. Nicolas shouts out, "Léon! *Ah! Quel bon garçon!* Such a good boy!"

Léon looks surprised at the sound of his name echoing through the stable. He looks up at the gathering. A moment of confusion on his face. I walk toward him slowly, without threat.

Léon speaks. His voice is thick with the nasal sounds of French pronunciation.

"*Mon papa,* he is very not correct. Very bad I am with the English," says Léon with the forced trace of a smile.

"I'm surprised to hear you say that. You spoke such fine English when I first came in. To quote, 'I'm tremendously happy' and 'It's been quite a ride.' Now that's impressive, excellent…impeccable English, each word used properly, spoken properly."

At first it seems as if he's going to remain silent. But he's a smart lad. Smart enough to trust his own brain. He speaks.

"You know how, *monsieur,* in the classes of English they teach first the American conversational English. The idiom expressions. *Oui.* It is a challenge they teach me good."

I interrupt.

"Did they teach you to say 'I'd like to bet ten grand on Rufus' or 'I'd like to place twenty thousand on Millie's Baby Boy'? How did you learn that?"

He is now a frightened little boy.

I snatch the phone from his hand. I find the last message sent and I read out loud the recipient: "starsbook472ko.com."

Then, holding the phone above my head, I say to the crowd, "It appears that Léon and I use the same bookie. Only this time Léon is betting *against* the horse his father rides."

I hand the cell phone to K. Burke. She looks at the screen and shakes her head.

"Jesus Christ!" she says. "Who would have thought?"

I move in, close to Léon. Then I speak. Directly to Léon.

"First, you thought you'd spread a rumor to get longer odds on Garçon. But you realized you stood to earn more from sabotaging and betting against the expected winners. How could you do this? To your father? To the Savatiers? How could you hurt and betray the best people in your life?"

K. Burke gets it, too. Her mind works fast.

"You needed the money, Léon, didn't you?" I say.

Burke begins explaining—in French—to Armand Joscoe and Madame and Monsieur Savatier what has happened.

Léon is the person who sent the threats and the arrangements of roses to Marguerite. Who murdered the training horse. That Léon threatened the Savatiers and told them to order his father to lose.

"Léon would make a fortune if Garçon lost this race," I add. "Though he wanted Garçon to win the Preakness—and knew he could, due to his father, since Garçon runs very well in mud—so that the bets would be sky-high for this final race in the Triple Crown."

The Savatiers' faces are saturated with shock, horror, and confusion. How could such a thing be? How could someone so close to them execute a scheme so hideous? They simply don't understand such an evil world.

Armand's face also looks sad, then horrified, and then…his face quickly turns to a red and wild rage.

"Comment as-tu pu?" he screams it over and over. How could you? How could you?

"J'ai le diable pour fils!" he screams. I have the devil for a son!

K. Burke and I move to either side of Léon.

Armand also moves closer to his son. He faces Léon. Tears are rolling down Armand's cheeks. I am expecting the symbolic slap across the face.

But there is no slap. Instead Armand moves swiftly. He throws his fist up high. That fist travels to his son's jaw with enormous force and a great cracking sound. Léon falls to the floor of the stable. He moans.

Armand looks down at his son and spits, then he screams and runs from the stable.

CHAPTER 36

Belmont.
Race Day.

AT TEN IN THE morning, Marguerite and Nicolas Savatier, K. Burke, and I watch a young Cuban jockey taking Garçon on a gallop around a training track. Also watching the "audition" of the replacement jockey are assorted trainers, sports writers, Belmont officials, and even four competing jockeys. Garçon appears relaxed and ready.

"Que pensez-vous, mes amis?" I say to the owners. What do you think of it, my friends?

"He will have to do," says Nicolas.

Marguerite says what we are all thinking. "It is a tragedy. To come this far. To be this close. The Triple Crown within sight…"

The most senior of the Belmont officials says, "You can still withdraw the horse, Mrs. Savatier. It's happened before."

"No. I could not do that to Garçon. My wonderful horse has waited all his life for this," says Marguerite.

Everyone present has a point of view. One of the trainers thinks the Cuban jockey is "almost as good as Armand." Another thinks the Cuban jockey is *"trop rapide avec la cravache."*

"Okay, Moncrief. I can't translate that one," K. Burke says.

"The jockey is 'too quick with the riding crop,'" I answer.

The talk grows faster, more passionate. I hear Marguerite say, "Garçon will race even if I have to ride him myself."

Then I watch Nicolas look toward the vibrant blue sky and say, *"Aidez-moi, s'il vous plaît, mon cher Dieu."* Please help me, dear God.

Then a man's voice comes from behind us. Startling all of us.

It is sudden and strong.

"Who is riding my horse?" he shouts.

The voice belongs to Armand Joscoe.

"Armand…" says Marguerite. "We have not seen you since yesterday. We had no idea where you were."

Armand tells us that since yesterday morning he has been dealing with the Belmont New York police, as well as an assistant New York State attorney general, two representatives of the New York State Racing Commission, two attorneys who represent Belmont Park, and a son who has committed a serious and unforgivable crime.

Quickly Marguerite interrupts.

"No," she says. "Nothing is so serious that it cannot be forgiven."

"So true. So true," says Nicolas. "You are here with us now. We shall all be friends once again. You will see."

The Cuban jockey has alighted from Garçon. Armand Joscoe rushes toward "his" horse. Then he shouts for the trainers.

"Get the drying cloths immediately. He's wet. Walk him slowly. Cool him down. Feed him half of his usual food. Get him inside. Hurry!"

The only way to describe the faces of Marguerite and Nicolas is "joyful."

I turn to my partner.

"So, what do you think, K. Burke?"

"Well, with all the Savatiers' talk about forgiveness and everyone being friends again, I can only think one thing: those two would never make it in New York City."

I laugh and say, "K. Burke, *vous êtes un biscuit dur.*"

She smiles, but not with her eyes. "Not as tough a cookie as I seem."

CHAPTER 37

Belmont.
The race.

K. BURKE, NICOLAS AND Marguerite Savatier, Luc Moncrief. Together again at a horse race, for the third time.

In the owners' circle. The weather is perfect, even cool for summer. We are all tense, tired, a little shaky from raw nerves and too many glasses of pre-race champagne.

"You know, K. Burke, two years ago, when American Pharoah won this race, it had been almost forty years since any horse had captured the Triple Crown. The wise guys, the smart money, 'the horse guys,' they all say it will be another forty years before it happens again. They have weighed the odds. They know the facts. I worry for Garçon's chances."

Burke makes a skeptical face.

"That's what 'the horse guys' say. I guess I'm getting more and more like you, Moncrief. I say, 'Don't always go with the facts. Sometimes you have to go with your heart.'"

Nicolas has been listening to our conversation.

"My heart says that I am enormously grateful that Armand has returned to the job of jockey. You know, I don't really care if Garçon wins the race."

"Don't be insane, Nicolas. I certainly care," says Marguerite.

"Indeed, feel however you like. I care enough for the both of us."

The four of us could easily banter and bicker until night falls, but the trumpet blows. The horses assemble within the starting gate. Of course, our attention is focused on Garçon. He seems under control, calm. I glance at Millie's Baby Boy. He's equally calm. Rufus, the only other real contender, is skittish.

The gun.

The race.

The cheers.

I am no expert at calling races, but from the start we all can see that it's going to be close. Garçon and Millie's Baby Boy take the lead together. They are, as the inevitable saying goes, neck-in-neck. So close that the two riders could carry on a conversation.

As always, Burke is amazingly excited. She shouts. "Hey, Millie, get off Garçon's ass!"

The two horses seem almost to run as a team. But then…as they close in on the finish, I am ecstatic to see that Millie's Baby Boy is falling behind. Not behind a great deal at first. Just a bit. Then a length. Then perhaps three lengths.

But now…as they approach the finish…What should be a glorious win for Garçon turns into a problem.

From fifth-in-the-pack, Rufus has become Garçon's new partner.

And now…and now…

My eyes cannot see even a slight difference as they cross the finish line.

Different people erupt with different shouts. Rufus! Garçon! Rufus! Garçon! An announcement. The crowd quiets.

The photo sign will be posted and the results will be announced.

The waiting, of course, feels like a few hundred lifetimes.

The crowd turns even quieter.

Video screens play the finish over and over.

Finally, a voice echoes out of the loudspeakers:

"The winner, by a head, is Garçon."

EPILOGUE

K. BURKE AND I are together in Paris.

Why Paris? Because the Savatiers have decided to forgo the final important race in America, the Breeders' Cup. Instead, Garçon has been brought home to Paris to compete in the most important of French races, *Le Prix de l'Arc de Triomphe.*

Why together?

Frankly, because I find it impossible now to be in Paris without her. After our previous visits, visits that were touched with both tragedy and tenderness, Katherine Burke has given me new eyes to see Paris, from the glamorous shops on the Champs-Élysées to that perfect little bistro in Montmartre.

Burke and I are walking slowly through the Bois de Boulogne, the great forest-like park on the outskirts of Paris. It is also in the Bois where Parisians keep their own famous racetrack, Longchamp.

"Leave it to the French to build a racetrack smack dab in the middle of a beautiful park," says K. Burke.

"The park is for *fun*. The track is for *games*. Fun and games," I say.

"Whatever you say. Anyway, I'm always happy to be here," she says.

"And you will be even happier if tomorrow Garçon wins."

"Yes, I will. Especially that it's my own one hundred euros that I bet on him."

We walk without speaking for a few minutes.

It is October in Paris. Usually a rainy time of the year. But today the air is cool and the sky is bright. The trees are dripping with color—autumn reds and yellows.

"I hope the weather will be this great tomorrow," I say.

We are now walking so close to each other that our shoulders occasionally touch, our hands occasionally brush against each other's.

"And if the weather isn't so great, at least we're in Paris," she says.

"You have grown to like this city, eh, K. Burke?"

"I've grown to *love* this city," she says.

"Maybe we should both move here, live here," I say.

"If you'd said that a year ago I would simply say that you're crazy," she says. "But now I almost feel the same way."

I stop. I talk.

"That means we have become crazy together."

She says, "So now we're *both* crazy. I guess that's good."

I take her hand. We continue our walk.

ABOUT THE AUTHORS

JAMES PATTERSON has written more bestsellers and created more enduring fictional characters than any other novelist writing today. He lives in Florida with his family.

RICHARD DiLALLO is a former advertising creative director. He has had numerous articles published in major magazines. He lives in Manhattan with his wife.

BONJOUR, DETECTIVE LUC MONCRIEF.
NOW WATCH YOUR BACK.

Very handsome and charming French detective Luc Moncrief
joined the NYPD for a fresh start—but someone
wants to make his first big case his last.

Welcome to New York.

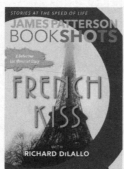 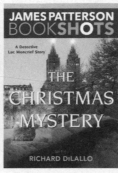 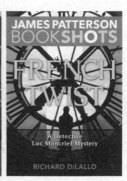

Read all the heart-pounding thrillers
in the Luc Moncrief series:

French Kiss
The Christmas Mystery
French Twist

Available only from

BOOK**SHOTS**

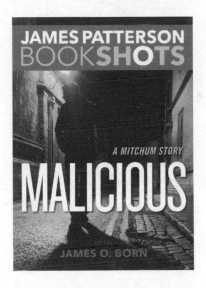

HARRY POSEHN IS THE BEST DAD, THE BEST HUSBAND ... WELL, MAYBE NOT.

Detective Teaghan Beaumont is getting closer and closer to discovering the truth about Harry Posehn. But there's a twist that she—and you, dear reader—will never see coming.

Can Beaumont catch him before it's too late? Read *The House Husband*, available only from

BOOK**SHOTS**

HER HUSBAND HAS A TERRIBLE SECRET....

Miranda Cooper's life takes a terrifying turn when an SUV
deliberately runs her family's car off a desolate Arizona road. With
her husband badly wounded, she must run for help alone as his
cryptic parting words echo in her head: "Be careful who you trust."

**Read the heart-pounding thriller, *Come and Get Us*,
available now from**

BOOK**SHOTS**

GOD SAVE THE QUEEN—ONLY PRIVATE CAN SAVE THE ROYAL FAMILY.

Private is the most elite detective agency in the world. But when kidnappers threaten to execute a royal family member in front of the Queen, Jack Morgan and his team have just twenty-four hours to stop them. Or heads will roll…literally.

Read the brand-new addition to the Private series,
Private: The Royals, **available only from**

BOOKSHOTS

IS HARRIET BLUE AS TALENTED A DETECTIVE AS LINDSAY BOXER?

Harriet Blue, the most single-minded detective since Lindsay Boxer, won't rest until she stops a savage killer targeting female university students. But new clues point to a more chilling predator than she could ever have imagined….

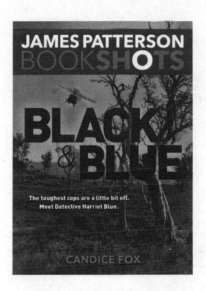

Will Harriet solve the case before time runs out?
Read *Black & Blue,* available only from

BOOK**SHOTS**

THE GREATEST STORY IN MODERN HISTORY
HAS A NEW CHAPTER....

Posing as newlyweds, two ruthless thieves board the *Titanic* to rob its well-heeled passengers. But an even more shocking plan is afoot—a sensational scheme that could alter the fate of the world's most famous ship.

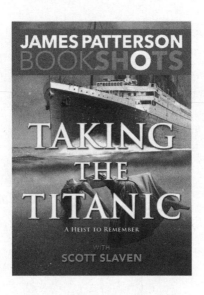

The world's most famous ship lives again in this thrilling tale, *Taking the Titanic,* available only from

BOOK**SHOTS**

"I'M NOT ON TRIAL. SAN FRANCISCO IS."

Drug cartel boss the Kingfisher has a reputation for being violent and merciless. And after he's finally caught, he's set to stand trial for his vicious crimes—until he begins unleashing chaos and terror upon the lawyers, jurors, and police associated with the case. The city is paralyzed, and Detective Lindsay Boxer is caught in the eye of the storm.

Will the Women's Murder Club make it out alive—or will a courtroom shocker ensure their last breaths?

Read the shocking new Women's Murder Club story, available only from

BOOK**SHOTS**

HE'S WORTH MILLIONS…
BUT HE'S WORTHLESS WITHOUT HER.

Siobhan Dempsey came to New York with a purpose: she wants to become a successful artist. But then she meets tech billionaire Derick Miller, who takes her breath away. And though Siobhan's body comes alive at his touch, their relationship has been a roller-coaster ride.

Are they meant to be together?

Read the steamy Diamond Trilogy books:

Dazzling: The Diamond Trilogy, Book I
Radiant: The Diamond Trilogy, Book II
Exquisite: The Diamond Trilogy, Book III

Available only from